Helen Dunmore

Zillah & Me

SCHOLASTIC
PRESS

Scholastic Children's Books,
Commonwealth House, 1–19 New Oxford Street,
London WC1A 1NU, UK
a division of Scholastic Ltd
London ~ New York ~ Toronto ~ Sydney ~ Auckland
Mexico City ~ New Delhi ~ Hong Kong

First published in the UK by Scholastic Ltd, 2000

ISBN 0 439 01298 8
ISBN 0 439 99718 6

Typeset by DP Photosetting, Aylesbury, Bucks.
Printed by Cox and Wyman Ltd, Reading, Berks.

10 9 8 7 6 5 4 3 2 1

Zillah
& Me

Also in Scholastic Press:

Madame Retsmah Predicts
Michael Coleman

Brother, Brother, Sister, Sister
Helen Dunmore

The Dragon Upstairs
My Second-Best Friend
Geraldine Kaye

Ice Cat
Linda Newbery

Firehead
K. M. Peyton

Harry and the Wrinklies
Ragboy, Rats and the Surging Sea
Alan Temperley

The Girl in the Blue Tunic
Whistle and I'll Come
Jean Ure

Chapter One

It's raining so hard I could write a message, put it in a bottle and throw it out of the window, and I'm sure it would float away. I wonder where the storm would take it? Maybe all the way back to London. I wonder if anyone would ever open it and read it.

Here I am, Katie Jenner, buried under the duvet, in my bedroom, in a cottage half a mile from the cliffs, just about to blow off the edge of Cornwall if this storm gets any worse.

Mum's asleep. How can she sleep? You can hear the thump of the sea on the cliffs. Punch, punch, punch, like a fight in a film. And the wind howling, and the rain spattering on the window. Or maybe it's hail.

At least it's warm in here, under the duvet. If you need the toilet you have to go downstairs, out of the back door, then down the path to the outside toilet at the bottom of the garden. Can you believe that we've come to live for a whole year in a cottage without an inside toilet? In fact there is no bathroom at all. There's a sink in the kitchen where we can wash, and a tin bath which Mum says we can fill with hot water from the stove.

"We'll light a fire, and have our baths in front of it. It'll be really cosy. Just imagine, Katie, a bath by firelight."

Hmm. I can see that we won't be having baths too often. I think of the power-shower in our house in London, and feel a pang of homesickness. My friends would kill me if they knew that the first thing I missed was the shower. But at least we've got running water, and electricity, so I can read in bed. Imagine if we only had candles...

But the outside toilet is going to be a problem. The spider angle was the first thing I checked out. My findings were:

1) an exceptionally large black spider crouched on top of the toilet door, ready to zoom down as soon as anyone got comfortable;
2) a nest of spiderlings in the corner, waiting to turn into large spiders and join their mum on top of the door;
3) (last-minute discovery) a small brown spider with very hairy legs crouched inside the toilet roll, waiting for me.

"MUM! Come and get the spiders out of here!"

Mum doesn't mind spiders. In fact, she is always helping them out of the bath so they can have a better life outside. But today, after driving the van with our stuff in it all the way from London, she wasn't feeling very sympathetic.

"Oh, Katie! You aren't going to fuss about spiders all the time, are you? We're in the country now. You'll just have to get used to them."

Mum's put one of Dad's old coats on the hook by the back door.

"Wrap that round yourself when you go out, Katie. Don't forget to put your boots on. The garden's full of stinging nettles."

This is true. There are even nettles growing *inside* the outside toilet, along with the spiders, slugs and tufts of grass.

"It's perfectly clean, Katie," Mum said hopefully, as she sloshed another bucket of Jeyes Fluid round the toilet floor, which looks as if it is made of earth. "But if you don't like it out here, you can always use the chamber-pot. I've left one under your bed."

Chamber-pot! I looked at Mum to see if she was joking, but she wasn't. It's exactly like doing the Victorians in Mrs Ellis's class. Except that we're not doing Victorian life, we're living it.

"That's OK, Mum. I don't really mind the nettles."

The wind howls, and the cottage rocks. It's only October. What's it going to be like in the middle of winter? It's all right for Mum – she *likes* weather. That's why we've come here. She's going to paint the weather. She's going to paint the rain and the sun and the hail and the snow and the way the light changes over everything when the clouds move. She's going to paint the light and the seasons and everything that happens in the whole year we're going to be here.

"You get all the weather in the world coming in from the sea," she said to me when we'd unloaded the van. Her face was flushed and her eyes were bright as if she was about to open the best present ever. "Look, Katie!"

She pointed out to sea, at a heap of black cloud that was moving fast, straight towards our cottage, where it was going to dump bucket-loads of rain on our heads if we didn't get indoors quickly.

"Oh, yes," I said. "Mmm. Looks good, Mum."

Because I couldn't spoil it for her. I hadn't seen Mum looking like this, full of life and almost hopeful, for months and months. Not since...

I'd better tell you about it. Nothing makes sense until you know. In one way it's hard to talk about it, but in another way it's easy. I only have to shut my eyes to see it all as clearly as if it was still happening, somewhere in a world which I can't get back to any more. But if I could press a rewind button, I would go back to the moment before anything happened. Then I'd pause the film and we'd stay there for ever, Mum still upstairs sorting out the laundry basket, me wandering out of the front door with a glass of orange juice because Jessie's phone was engaged and I was going to watch Dad for a few minutes before I tried her again, and Dad—

All of us happy without knowing we were happy, because we didn't even need to know.

What I see is a narrow terraced house in London: our house. In front of the house, jammed in by the front door, there's a sooty old lilac tree. It's grown much too big for the space, and we've got to do something about it. Dad wanted to cut it back himself. Mum wanted to get an expert to do it.

"Why don't you look in the Yellow Pages for someone who does trees?" she asked him.

"Yellow Pages!" Dad snorted. "Do you think I can't even cut a couple of branches off a lilac bush?"

The next thing we knew, he'd hired an electric saw and borrowed a ladder from Mr Riordan down the street. It was a steel ladder with lots of complicated safety locks on it.

I remember everything, so I must have been there. I *know* I was there. I can remember everything, only it's like watching a film. Not like a memory at all.

Dad put the ladder at the base of the lilac. Most lilacs are scrubby little bushes, but ours had grown into a big, tough tree, branching up into the sky. It was so big it had forgotten how to flower, and everyone said it was damaging the foundations of our house.

Dad must have propped the ladder up. It was a tall ladder, made in two parts, and you had to join them together with safety catches. I wasn't really looking just then. I had my yo-yo but I wasn't doing tricks with it or anything. Just looking up the street and letting the yo-yo run up and down the string. Out of the corner of my eye I must have seen Dad fiddling with the safety catches. I didn't know that Dad hadn't really understood when Mr Riordan explained how to set the ladder up safely. It took him a while to do it. Maybe he thought about going back up the street to ask Mr Riordan again, but he didn't. Maybe he thought it couldn't be *that* complicated. *I must have got it more or less right.* I can almost hear Dad thinking that.

Dad was near the top of the ladder when something happened. There was a crackling noise and I saw Dad still on the ladder, going backwards with it through the little branches. His hands grabbed out, but the air flew past them. And he yelled out one word with all his voice: "MAGGIE!"

That's Mum's name. By the time she ran out of the house, Dad had fallen. The ladder threw him off on to the concrete path that runs from our front door to the gate. Ran, I mean. I keep forgetting that we don't live there any more.

MAGGIE! His voice was gone, but I could still hear it. Dad was lying on his back on the concrete path, with his eyes open. He didn't see me. And then Mum was down beside him.

I remember that when we all went in the ambulance Mum kept saying, "He was only cutting back the lilac." As if that would make it all not true. People don't die in the middle of Saturday morning, because they've decided they'd better prune the lilac tree. But the ambulance went faster and faster, and I could hear the siren, only this time it wasn't somebody else being rushed to hospital, it was us.

When we talked about moving down here from London, Mum said, "It'll be good for us, Katie." She told me about how her old school-friend, Janice, had a cottage we could rent for hardly any money. (Janice married a Cornish farmer as soon as she left school, and as far as I know Mum hasn't seen her since the day of the wedding.) One day Janice was going to do up the cottage for holiday people, but she hadn't got round to it yet. "Just as well for us. It's a chance in a million," Mum said. "And there's a school in the next village. There's a school bus, Janice says. Her daughter goes on it. Just think, Katie, a year in the country, with the sea on our doorstep!" Mum made it sound as if living in Cornwall was the one thing she'd always wanted to do. But later on I heard her on the phone to her friend Bridget: "I've got to get away from this house. I can't go on living here. I can't sleep, I can't work."

So that's why I'm here, huddled up under the duvet, in my new bedroom in a cottage at the edge of the cliffs, in Cornwall, Great Britain, the World, the Universe. Because of a lilac tree.

Chapter Two

I heard Zillah's voice before I knew who she was. It must have been about nine o'clock, and I'd only just woken up. The storm was over, and the sky was a pale, clear blue, with thin white clouds racing over it. We hadn't put the curtains up yet, so I lay on my back and watched the sky and thought about getting up and helping Mum unpack the rest of the boxes. I could hear her moving about downstairs. The cottage is so small you can hear every sneeze.

My new bedroom is tiny, but I like the way the window is tucked deep into the wall. Unless you're in bed, you have to bend down to look out of it. The plaster is uneven, and the walls bulge outwards. Mum told me that they had to build cottages with thick walls round here, or they wouldn't last through the winters. So I was lying there, warm and sleepy, not moving in case Mum heard me and made me get up and start my new life. *My duvet is my only home,* I thought, and I nearly laughed.

That was when I heard Zillah. Her voice came as close and clear as if she was in the room with me.

"I'm going back. I don't want to meet some stupid girl from London."

"Oh no, you're not, young lady, and you can take that look off your face. And don't dare drop those eggs or you'll pay for them out of your pocket money."

It sounded like part of a long argument that went on most of the time, and even though they were bored with it, still they went on nagging.

"And I'm not sitting with her on the school bus. I don't sit with *anyone* on the school bus. I've got my own place."

"I know you have," sighed her mum. "And I wish you hadn't. Why have you always got to be difficult, Zillah? Why can't you try to be friends, like everyone else?"

Zillah! Maybe her mum had chosen the wrong name, if she wanted her to be just like everyone else. Now they were quarrelling right under my window. I lay tight, frozen in case they saw me. But of course they couldn't. And then they went nagging off towards the front door, and a moment later I heard Mum's voice, all warm and pleased and surprised.

"Janice! How wonderful! Oh dear, you haven't changed at all. I'd have recognized you anywhere."

And then there was a murmuring, hugging noise

and Janice said in a quite different voice, not snappy or naggy at all, "Oh Maggie, what a time it's been. And so much happening to us both. Who'd have believed it? Well, thank God we can't see into our own futures. Oh, I'm sorry, Maggie dear, I didn't mean to upset you, I was always the clumsy one."

"It's all right, you haven't upset me. I'd rather talk about it. It's so much better than when people pretend nothing's happened."

"Don't tell me. *Lovely weather we're having, my dear, and let's not mention your husband.* People can be very cruel, without meaning to be."

Janice spoke as if she knew what she was talking about. I wondered if anything had happened to Janice's husband.

Then Mum said eagerly, "And who's this? Is this your daughter, Janice? She must be. She looks just like you used to."

"Yes," said Janice, in a funny, cross way, as if she wanted to be proud of Zillah but couldn't be. "This is my Zillah."

"It's lovely to meet you, Zillah. You must be just the same age as Katie. She'll be so glad to find a friend on the doorstep."

And that's as well as having the sea on my doorstep, I thought, dragging on my jeans and a sweatshirt. Any minute now Mum would be bound to call me down to meet my new friend.

Sometimes I really wish adults could have the experience of being introduced in the same way as children.

"Mrs Jones, meet Mr Carter. He's thirty-six, just like you! Off you go and play together, you're bound to make friends."

"Oh, there you are, Katie. I was just going to call you. Look, this is Zillah. She's the same age as you, and you're going to be in the same class."

I smiled, and Zillah shook her hair further over her face and scowled at me through it.

"Zillah!" said her mother sharply.

"Hi," I said. "Sorry, I'm not very awake yet. You must be Janice, Mum's friend."

I wanted them to stop looking at Zillah. It would only make things worse. But Janice didn't seem to care about that.

"Zillah! Say hello to Katie this minute!"

Zillah shot me a look of pure hatred and muttered. "Hello, *Katie*."

"Why don't you two go and have a look around?" Mum suggested. "Katie's hardly had a chance to see anything yet. We've been unpacking since we got here."

"And I'm so sorry I wasn't here to meet you," said Janice. "But I had to go to Truro to see Geoff's cousin – she's not well, you know –"

"I know. *Families*," said Mum sympathetically. "Yes, go out for a bit with Zillah, Katie. Remember we're going to paint the sitting-room later."

Janice stared at her. "Paint the sitting-room?"

"Yes. White," said Mum firmly. "I need more light. That's where I'm going to paint, at least when the weather's bad. Of course I'll be working outside a lot."

"Of course," echoed Janice faintly.

"We can get the painting done today. Katie's a star with a roller, and we've brought the paint with us."

Janice still looked disbelieving. I wish she'd seen my bedroom in London. I painted it all myself. Sea-green walls, white ceiling, marine blue on the door. I even did some stencilling round the window-frame, in a pattern of shells. It took the whole weekend, but Jessie came over and helped, and we had a brilliant time. *And* I did most of the kitchen, and the bathroom – with a bit of help from Mum. Mum always says I'm very practical, like her, not like–

Mustn't think about that.

Zillah was looking at me curiously. For a moment she had forgotten to scowl.

"Go *on*, Zillah! Don't stand there like a dowsy!" said her mum, and with the scowl locked back on her face like a mask, Zillah pushed past me out of the kitchen door. I followed. The wind was still so strong that it half-blew me down the path, but the

13

sun was bright and it wasn't cold. Everything looked completely different in the sun. Shadows raced over the little fields, and down below the sea glittered. But Zillah was going so fast I'd have to run to catch up with her. I ran. That's another thing Zillah didn't know: I'm in the junior cross-country team at my school. My old school. You might not think there's much country to cross in the middle of London, but that doesn't stop us. Zillah wasn't expecting me to shoot past her and block the way.

"OK," I said. "We don't have to be friends. But we'd better pretend today, or your mum will go crazy again."

"I'm not your friend," said Zillah. I sighed.

"That's what I just said. You don't have to be. Just show me a few things, and we can go back to the cottage and everyone'll be happy. Then I can get on with painting the sitting-room for Mum."

"You really going to paint that whole room? Let her do it herself, I would."

Yeah, I bet you would, I thought. But maybe it wasn't Zillah's fault that she hated her mum. Her mum didn't seem to be too nice to her.

"Is there a way down the cliffs, to the beach?" I asked. "Mum told me there's a beach."

Zillah looked at me as if I was an idiot. "Yeah, if you want to get drowned. Can't you see it's high tide? And there's a big sea running."

"After the storm, you mean?"

"Storm! That wasn't a storm. Just a bit of a blow," said Zillah scornfully. "You wait till winter comes, then you'll see storms. Spray comes up and covers the windows so all you see's a salt crust. You get blown over going up the lane for the school bus."

After that she wouldn't talk any more. We walked across the fields, scrambling over little falling-down walls. My hair blew into my eyes so I couldn't see where I was going, and I stepped in a cow-pat, which made Zillah smile for the first time. There were thistles and nettles everywhere, which was fine for Zillah, as she was wearing boots. The wind went roaring over the land and there in front of us was a stretch of tumbled rocks and short grass.

"Cliff edge," said Zillah reluctantly, as if she'd thought about not telling me, so I could walk straight over it. I went slowly forward. The wind was behind me, pushing me. I could see for miles, right down to the end of Cornwall, maybe. The cliffs bulked over the sea, all the way down the coast. Black rocks stuck out of the water, with white foam crawling round them. There were birds flying, diving down into the wildness of the waves, then pulling themselves up and screeching into the wind. The sea shocked against the cliffs. They weren't white cliffs like the ones I'd seen at Dover, when we went to France on the ferry. They were grey and heavy, and old. As if they'd been there for ever, fighting the sea. I went forward a little farther, and peered down.

There was the water, boiling into the cove. I couldn't imagine ever swimming there. And the black rocks sticking up like spikes, ready to stab through you if you fell.

If you fell. Hundreds of metres on to rock. Rock as hard as concrete. Fell with your hands stretched out, reaching for nothing. Like—

I stumbled back, away from the edge. Zillah was looking at me, with a little smile edging her lips.

"Don't like heights, then?" she asked. "You better not think about climbing down to the beach, even when the tide's out. Don't want to go losing you now, do we, *Katie*?"

I knew she was trying to make me angry, but I wasn't going to be angry. If she'd hated being with me that much, she'd have run off as soon as we were out of sight of the cottage and Mum and Janice. But she hadn't. She was staring at the sea, drinking in the sight of it.

"It's beautiful here," I said.

Zillah shot me a look. Not angry any more, not scowling. Really looking at me for a moment. As if she was trying to find out what I was like.

"Yeah," she said. "Not like London, eh?"

"No. Not like London."

"Sorry," said Zillah. "I didn't mean – I mean, I know London's your home."

"Not any more," I said. Janice must have told her about Dad.

That's why she said "Sorry" like that. Usually I hate it when people talk about Dad dying, and being sorry. But Zillah sounded different. Almost as if she knew what it was like. I glanced at her curiously. She was looking at me. She wanted to know about me, just as I wanted to know about her. Then she looked away.

"Got to go," she muttered.

"See you," I said. I wondered if I would, except at school, or when Janice forced her to come down to the cottage again. I could just imagine Janice dragging Zillah down the lane, saying, "You *will* be friends with Katie! You *will* be friends with Katie!" It wasn't a great start to making friends. Still ... you never know...

Chapter Three

Mum's just made me a big mug of hot chocolate. We've finished the sitting-room: walls, ceiling, door, window-frame, everything. It's past ten o'clock. Mum did the ceiling, and I did the rest while she finished the unpacking and worked out how to light the kitchen stove, according to Janice's instructions. (The house quickly filled with smoke, and I started screaming at Mum to open the door in case the new paintwork turned grey.)

We pulled out the stinky old carpet before we started, and threw it away. Janice said she'd meant to do it before we came, but there'd been a crisis with the turkeys and she hadn't had time. The turkeys are meant to be fattening up for Christmas, but unfortunately they keep dying, and Janice is desperate, Mum says, because the turkey money is very important. Maybe that's what makes her so cross. Underneath the carpet, the floor was stone. Mum scrubbed it, and when she gets some money she's going to buy some matting to put down.

"It's going to be perfect," she said. But I know what it's really going to be like, and perfect isn't quite the right word, unless you are Mum. There'll be a smell of paint and turps and there'll be brushes and charcoal and acrylics and palettes everywhere, on top of the big chest where Mum keeps her work in long flat drawers. Mum is actually quite organized, but it's her own sort of organization. There'll be the radio on loud, and half-drunk mugs of coffee in the corners of the room, where she thinks she won't trip over them, and packets of polos and Milka chocolate because Mum won't stop for lunch, not even a sandwich, when things are going well. And there'll be a guilty smell of cigarettes because Mum has to have "just one to get me started". I hate her smoking. When I smell the smoke I want to scream at her, "Don't do it! Don't you know you could die?"

But I don't, because I know she's trying. She keeps saying to me, "Just don't ever start, Katie. It's fatal."

And it's Sunday night, and tomorrow I've got to go to school, in the school bus, with Zillah. At least she's not calling for me. We're to meet up at the bus stop in the village. I wonder if Zillah has any friends? Will the others think I'm like her, because our mothers are friends? Or will they all be like Zillah? Maybe Zillah is normal for Cornwall.

To calm myself down, I start to make lists in my head.

<u>Good things about Cornwall so far:</u>
Mum looking happy a bit of the time
Mum wanting to get started with her work tomorrow
Mum's studio now it's painted and we've thrown away
the carpet
my bedroom (though it needs painting)
Janice (possibly)
the sea (possibly, if I can ever get down to the beach)
no lilac tree

<u>Bad things about Cornwall so far:</u>
Zillah
the cliffs
Janice (possibly, if she is always as cross as this)
no Jessie
no friends
no shops
no McDonald's, Burger King, Pizza Hut etc etc
no phone (we can use the phone at the farm in
emergencies, or there's a call-box in the village)
IMAGINE HAVING NO PHONE
no power-shower, washbasin, bath etc
spiders
nettles
thistles
cow-pats
the outside toilet
Zillah (she's so bad she should be on the list twice)

Chapter Four

I've never been so tired in my life. I fell asleep in the school bus on the way home, as it bounced round all the villages, dropping kids off at farms and outlying cottages. My eyes kept closing. I would have slept past our stop if Susie Buryan hadn't leaned over the back of the seat and woken me up.

"Katie! You've got to get off here!" And then she said loudly, as Zillah came past, "Don't reckon *you'd* have bothered about Katie, would you, Zillah Treliske?"

I stumbled down the aisle of the bus after Zillah.

Later on, Mum said, "You're bound to be tired, Katie. It's like the first day of a new job. You feel as if everyone's watching you to see if you get it right or wrong. But did you like them? Do you think you're going to make friends there?"

"I don't know," I said slowly. "I mean – they're nice. But it's all so different."

But I couldn't explain to Mum how different it really is. First of all, there are only sixty-eight of us in the whole school, and that's counting the babies in reception. There'd only be about ten people in my class, if they arranged the classes by age. So there are two infant classes, and two junior classes.

The head-teacher teaches us: he's called Mr Trevelyan. He's nice, and strange at the same time. He seems to be completely obsessed by computers. "We may be a little country school but we're linked to the whole world through the Internet. Every child here has their own e-mail address! Now then, Katie, let's sort you out. I expect you'll be wanting to keep in touch with your old school in London. What's their e-mail address?"

"Umm ... sorry, Sir, I don't really know..."

Mr Trevelyan's eyes flashed with excitement. "We can soon find out for you! Perhaps we can set up an on-line geography project!"

Mr Trevelyan lives in a house next to the school, with two little kids and a baby. We can see the little kids whizzing round the garden on their trikes, or whacking each other with spades in their sandpit, while we're in the playground. If they see Mr Trevelyan they start yelling, "Daddy!" Sometimes, Susie says, he lets them come into the school garden. The Trevelyans also keep goats, and grow all their own organic vegetables.

Apart from Susie, I made friends with a girl called

Bryony, and her twin brother Mark, who is in Top Group as well. (You don't have to be clever to be in Top Group, you just have to be in your last year of juniors.)

It was strange at dinner-time, when Zillah walked off on her own and sat against the playground wall, reading. It was the way she went off, not looking at anyone, as if there was no chance that she would ever have a friend. She tucked her coat under her and sat with her knees drawn up, leaning the book against them. All hunched up, not letting anybody in. And no one seemed to expect anything else. The little ones raced round, and the boys were playing football. Susie and some of the others were asking me about London. They didn't even look at Zillah. Suddenly I had a panicky feeling. The school bus had gone such a roundabout way that I didn't really know where I was. I certainly didn't know how to get back to the cottage. And this wasn't London, with buses and Tubes to take you home any time you wanted to go. What if the others didn't like me, either, once I'd stopped being new and interesting? What if they left me on my own, crouched up against the wall of the playground, pretending not to care? Zillah *must* be pretending.

But the school bus came safely, on time, to take us all home. I think that's why I'm tired, because all the time I was smiling and trying to get to know every-one, I was thinking about being stuck there for ever, unable to get home.

Mum had laid her charcoal sketches down in a circle. I looked from one to the next, and then at Mum. There were fierce swirls of cloud coming in over black sea, like a whirlwind. The land was tiny, crouching at the bottom of the paper.

"They're just sketches," said Mum, sweeping them together. "I'm going to spend tomorrow walking. I need to get the feel of the landscape. It's so long since I've been here."

"So long since you've been here?"

"Not since I was twelve," said Mum absently.

"I didn't know you'd been here before."

"Of course you did. You knew I always went on holiday with Janice."

"Yes – but I didn't know it was here."

"Well, it was a few miles away, beyond St Just. Janice's family took the same cottage every year, and they always asked me. Janice kept on coming, until she left home. That's how she met Geoff, at a dance in St Just."

"Why did you stop coming?"

"Oh, I don't know. Yes, I do. I was learning French at school and I really loved it. I got a French pen-friend and she asked me to Roscoff in the summer. And somehow I never came here again. But I always remembered it."

"Is it the same as you remembered?"

"No, not really. But then I'm older, and I've changed. I hadn't remembered how beautiful it was."

"Beautiful!"

"Yes, beautiful. Can't you see that, Katie?"

We were sitting in the kitchen, by the stove. Mum thinks she's learned to make it work now, but it's not very hot, and it still belches out smoke when the wind blows the wrong way down the chimney. The kitchen is quite dark and smoky and there's a stone sink, a wooden table, and a dresser with wonky shelves and metal hooks to hang cups. Mum has picked some Michaelmas daisies and put them on the table. But she didn't manage to cook anything, because the stove didn't get hot enough, so we had bread and ham and oranges.

After our supper, Mum and I started trying to heat up water for me to have a bath. She found a witch's cauldron in the outhouse, and we both scrubbed it out, then filled it up with cold water. It took two of us to hoist it on to the top of the stove, then Mum got the tin bath down, and rigged up a clothes horse round it, lined with towels, "to keep the draughts off". (Draught = the gale that blows under the kitchen door.)

But the water wouldn't heat. Mum peered into the belly of the stove.

"I think it's going out!" she said. "But I put loads of coke in. It should burn for hours. I know, I'll leave the back door open. Maybe that'll make it burn better."

She flung open the door and a gust of icy wind and rain blew in, making the cups rattle, and blowing Mum's sketches all over the kitchen.

"Oh no! Quick, Katie, catch them before they blow out of the door!"

The stove let out a belch of black smoke, and Mum slammed the door shut again.

"Hell! Hell! Hell!" Mum swore. "I wonder if Janice would mind you going up there for a bath."

"You can forget that, Mum. I am *certainly* not having a bath in Zillah's bathroom."

"All right, all right. Let's try this." Mum grabbed a sheet of newspaper, opened the stove door, and held the newspaper across the dying fire. Nothing happened.

"I give up," said Mum, sitting back on her heels. "I could *kick* this thing. Janice told me it worked beautifully."

"Well, she was lying."

At that moment, as if she had heard, Janice knocked on the door. We didn't know it was her, of course, so I started trying to shove away the clothes horse and the tin bath, just in case it was someone from school (though Susie Buryan lives two miles away).

"Janice!" said Mum. "Do you know how this (more swearing) thing works?"

Janice looked surprised at the sight of Mum smeared with soot and red with rage.

"But you haven't got the damper out," she said. "With the wind in the east like this, you've got to have the damper out."

"Thank you, Janice," said Mum, through gritted teeth.

"And you've put far too much coke in. You'll never get it going like that."

Janice knelt down and shovelled about inside the stove, emptying lukewarm coke back into the bucket. She riddled a poker around, then pulled out some knobs on the front of the stove.

"Right!" she said to the stove. "No more of your tricks."

The stove was clearly terrified of Janice. In a few minutes it began to glow. After a quarter of an hour it was too hot to touch, and the water was beginning to get warm in the cauldron.

"Now you can let the damper in, bit by bit. Put a load of coke on before you go to bed, and it'll last all night. You won't have any problems once you get used to it."

"You're an angel, Janice," said Mum, who had gone back to her normal colour.

"You'll be wanting fires in the bedrooms, too, to get the damp out of the cottage. Use coal for those, not coke – it's on the left-hand side of your coal bunker. And Geoff'll get you a load of logs. There's plenty of driftwood down on the beach, as well."

Fires in the bedrooms! I've always wanted a real fire in my bedroom, like in stories.

"Katie'll be able to do that, I'm sure," said Janice, looking at me kindly. "I heard about you painting the sitting-room. You must be a great help to your mother. I wish my Zillah was more like you!"

I was glad Zillah wasn't there to hear that. It would make her hate me more than ever.

"I'll leave you in peace to have your bath," said Janice. "I only came down to bring you these potatoes."

She'd dropped a sack by the door as she came in. It was full of enormous, mud-clodded potatoes. They looked like a different species from the clean, pale potatoes Mum buys in the supermarket.

"Wonderful!" said Mum. "You've saved my life, Janice. We'll have baked potatoes tomorrow, Katie."

"Can I really have a fire in my bedroom, Mum?" I asked as soon as Janice had gone.

28

"Yes, why not? Janice says the chimneys have been swept. Listen, I'll fill the coal-bucket. You take some newspaper and kindling-wood upstairs."

Mum was excellent at making the fire. She rolled up the newspapers and twisted them into circles, then laid the kindling on top in a tent shape.

"I do know how to do this. They always had open fires at Janice's cottage."

Then she put little bits of the driest coal on top.

"As soon as the wood gets going, put on more bits of coal with the tongs, Katie."

Mum lit the newspaper coils. The flames were tiny at first, flickering blue along the edge of the paper. Suddenly the draught caught them, and they began to run up the paper, straight and yellow. With a crackling noise, the wood caught fire. Carefully, I picked up the smallest bits of coal and placed them on top of the burning wood.

"That's it, keep going. Now some bigger bits."

It was lovely to see the fire leaping up. I turned off my light so there was only the firelight, with the flames changing from yellow to orange, and the fire settling as the paper burned away and the coal caught.

"I can't wait to go to bed," I said.

"Have your bath first. I've just tried the water: it's nearly boiling."

A bath you make yourself on top of a stove feels

like an adventure. You have to put cold water in the bottom of the bath first, then ladle in the hot, very carefully so it doesn't splash and scald you. Then, when the cauldron is half-empty and not too heavy, you can tip the rest in.

I had the warm stove on one side of my bath, and the clothes horse on the other to keep out the draughts. It was private and cosy, and Mum let me have some of her rose bath gel. There wasn't all that much water, and it wasn't all that hot, but it smelled fantastic. Mum even made me a cup of tea to drink in the bath. Mum said she'd empty the bath (you have to do it outside) because she didn't want me to get cold. I went straight upstairs and got into bed, and watched the shadows of the fire on the ceiling, and imagined I was living a hundred years ago. I could hear Mum next door, making a fire in her bedroom. It was like the first day of a holiday, with everything waiting to happen. Waiting ... as if we were waiting for something ... or someone.

Suddenly I knew who it was. What if Dad came in now, and saw the new white paint in the sitting-room, and the fire dancing, making patterns on the walls? What if he came quietly over to me and sat on the end of my bed, not saying anything, just being with me and enjoying the warmth of the fire?

"That's a great fire, Katie. I couldn't have done better myself."

The flames danced and dazzled. I held my breath, but nobody came.

Chapter Five

Thursday, October 31st, 8pm

Dear Jessie,

I wonder if it's as stormy as this in London? Mum has gone up to the farm. She's left me half a bar of chocolate, and I'm using her computer. But I can't do e-mail, because there's no phone.

I miss you loads. Tomorrow's Friday, and that's the end of my first week at school here. Mr Trevelyan (he's our teacher) says I am very capable but mentally lazy. Isn't it amazing, the things teachers think it's OK to say to you? But he's quite nice really, except that his brain is boiling over all the time, just like the pot of stew Mum left on top of the stove before she went out for a (very long) walk yesterday. Sometimes, to wake us up, Mr Trevelyan stamps up and down the classroom yelling, "Think! *Think!* THINK! Don't you realize that your brains are the most powerful computers anyone could imagine? If you had to buy them they would cost you hundreds of thousands of pounds!"

I've made a friend called Susie, and an enemy called Zillah. I wish it was the other way round – does that sound stupid? I like Susie, but. . .

Zillah has a boat of her own. It's a rowing boat with an outboard motor, and she keeps it in a cove a little way down the coast. She's allowed to take the boat out on her own. Our cove is no good for keeping a boat, because the sea covers it at high tide. But you can swim there at low tide, and fish from the rocks. It's sandy, and there's a deep rock-pool where you can swim when the sea's too rough. I haven't been down there yet – you have to climb a very steep path. If the weather's good at the weekend I'm going to go and explore it. Zillah's got her boat in a shed at the moment, because she's cleaning it and painting it ready for the winter. She hasn't told me this, because, as I said, she's my enemy and won't talk to me. But her mum says "That boat is the only thing Zillah cares about."

I wish you could hear the wind. And the sea. Those are the only sounds at night, apart from owls and foxes. Once I heard a screaming noise which I thought was a person, but Mum said it was a rabbit. There are no buses, no traffic, no trains, no ambulance sirens, no helicopters and no voices. We're at the bottom of the farm lane and no one comes down here. If you hear a sound, it's a cow in the field.

When I walk down the lane after school it's nearly dark, and the cows are being brought in for milking, so I have to squash up by the hedge. They make a soft snorting sound out of their noses at me. Stan (who brings the cows in) says they won't do you any harm, except you must never come between a cow and her calf.

Have you seen the people who are renting our house yet? What are they like? Please write straight away and tell me who's got my bedroom.

I miss you loads. (I think I've already said that.) Susie isn't a real friend, not like you. She might become one, but somehow I don't think so.

Lots of love, write soon,
Katie

PS Just off to the outside toilet with Mum's big torch.

Chapter Six

Saturday morning. Mum woke me, going out as soon as it was light, with her sketchbook wrapped in a plastic bag. I heard the door creak, her feet walking down the path, the swing of the wooden gate, then nothing. She'll be going to the cliffs. She said she was going to take photos, too. She's found a sheltered place, tucked into an overhang of rock, where she can look right down the coast, and out to sea.

"I'd love to build a little hut there," she said to me last night. "Right by the sea. Nothing but weather between me and America."

"Ireland," I said.

"What?"

"That's what's across the sea from us. Ireland. Not America."

"Mmm, yes, of course," said Mum vaguely. As she won't be drawing either of them, she doesn't really care a bit. "So you don't mind if I go out early, Katie? You can have a lie-in. But leave me a note if you go out, so I know where you are."

Mum is *so relaxed* here. In London, she had to know where I was every minute of the day. "*Don't call in to anyone's house on the way home from school, Katie! Or if you do, phone me. I need to know where you are.*" She wouldn't let me walk to school until I was nearly nine, because of the traffic. Not even with Jessie and Melanie. But here, I can go where I like. Mum has no worries about me falling off the cliff or being trampled by a herd of cows, or flattened by a milk lorry.

"It's safe here," she says. "People look out for one another, in the country."

Hmm. Still, I don't mind Mum letting me do whatever I want, and we're getting a lift into St Ives with Zillah's dad this afternoon. Our van keeps stalling because we need a new carburettor. The journey from London just about finished it off.

I haven't met Zillah's dad yet. We keep hearing about him, but we never see him. Very mysterious. I asked Mum what he was like (in case he was like Zillah) but she didn't seem too sure.

"Oh – I don't really know him, Katie. Of course I saw him at the wedding – and he was there the other night, but he didn't say much. He's got a lot on his mind. These are hard times for farmers, and they're having a struggle, from what Janice says."

I was lying there, thinking about all these things, when I heard the back door open. There was a stealthy little click, as if whoever had come in didn't want me to hear. Mum wouldn't open the door like that. I sat up in bed, my skin prickling. Very quietly, I swung my legs over the side of the bed, tiptoed to the door, and opened it. The noise came again. A soft sound of footsteps, inside this time.

"Maybe it's Janice," I told myself. If she knew Mum was out, she might not bother to knock. Maybe she'd brought some more potatoes. My heart was hammering and I felt hot all over, and sick, though I hadn't eaten anything yet.

"Janice!" I called. "Is that you? I'm coming down!" But my voice came out so high and trembling I wasn't sure it would even carry down the stairs. There was a long, mocking silence. I was really frightened now. If it wasn't Mum, and it wasn't Janice, who could it be? Suddenly the farm seemed miles away, not just up the lane. And we weren't even on the phone... Could I climb out of the window, and run? No, it was too high. I stared desperately round the room, looking for a weapon. The poker! Mum had left the poker in my room last night. I grabbed it and held it high, listening again. There was another faint sound from downstairs. I put my foot on the first tread of the staircase, then on the second. Slowly, silently, so they wouldn't creak. My right hand grasped the poker. Another step, and another, round the bend into the kitchen, and –

There was Zillah, sitting in one of our wooden chairs, her feet up on our table, smiling at me.

"What have you got the poker in your hand for, *Katie*?" she asked.

I was shaking and furious. I knew straight away that Zillah had frightened me on purpose, but she'd never admit it.

"I thought the stove might need a good poke," I said. "And take your feet off our table. We eat off there."

"Do you? *We* use plates," said Zillah. "I hope you don't mind me coming straight in. We always do that round here. Everyone leaves their doors open."

I didn't believe her. Janice always knocked, and she *owned* the cottage.

"What did you come for, anyway?"

"Mum says I've got to take you out. Show you the beach."

"You don't have to show me. I know where it is."

"The path's dangerous, unless you know it."

I'd never heard Zillah say so much. I looked at her closely, and wondered. Maybe she *did* want to be friends, in a strange Zillah type of way. The other day, she hadn't run off as soon as she got the chance.

And even though she doesn't talk to anyone at school, she must want to have friends, mustn't she?

"Or we could go and see my boat."

"I thought you were painting it."

"It's done. Might not get another fine day before the gales set in."

Suddenly I realized what was missing. The noise of the wind that had been beating around the cottage ever since we arrived, pushing in at the doors and windows. It had gone. The wind had sunk to nothing. It was a blue, still autumn day.

"Don't get many days like this," said Zillah again. "Might even take the boat out for a bit, if you're interested."

"I don't know, I—"

"Don't bother, then," snapped Zillah, swinging her legs off the table.

"I didn't mean I didn't want to, it's just – Wait a minute. Let me get my jacket."

We didn't talk as we went over the fields to the cliff. For the first time I could see why so many people wanted to come to Cornwall in summer. The sun dazzled me, and the sea shone like a silver plate. The breeze blew softly, smelling of salt and coconut, and I felt a big, stupid smile spreading over my face. I wanted to run, jump, shout out loud, sing. But as Zillah was walking in front of me, I wasn't going to.

Suddenly she turned round, and for the first time I saw the flash of a real smile, breaking up her face, changing it as the sun changed the wild landscape. A different Zillah, her twin sister.

"You see that path there? That's where you go down to the beach. But if you want to see my boat, we have to go on to the next cove."

I wanted *so much* to go down to the beach. I wanted to be down by the sea now, this minute, with the waves breaking in front of me and high cliffs behind me and gulls diving on to the water. But I didn't really want to go with Zillah. If she showed it to me for the first time, it would always be *her* beach, never mine. I'd be a visitor, and I was sick of being a visitor. Visitors never know anything, and they always have to be grateful to people for explaining what's going on. That's what it was like at school. I *was* grateful to Susie and the others. Susie was always showing me things, and telling me things. But I was tired of being new, nodding and saying, "Oh, yes, I see," when they told me all the stuff about homework, and the website Mr Trevelyan was designing, and how the school bus-driver hates kids (I had already worked this out on my own) and how we could grow our own vegetables in the school garden in summer. Organically, of course.

"Let's go to your boat," I said. Zillah smiled again, and set off fast along the path that runs near the edge of the cliffs. It's part of the Cornish Coastal Path, I think. You can walk hundreds of miles along the sea if you want. Imagine doing that, with a backpack and a map. The sea would be on one side, and the land on the other. I wonder if I'd get lonely, or frightened? Just walking on, not knowing what would be there around the next bend of the path. Mum would love it. Think of all the weather you'd see, walking round Cornwall. Maybe, one day, in summer, we could set out together...

"Come ON," yelled Zillah.

My legs were shaking by the time we got down to Zillah's cove. It was a steep climb, and Zillah went too fast for me to keep up with her. Her feet knew where to go, not like mine. She made it look as easy as running down the street. I slithered and lost my balance and nearly fell, and had to grab on to clumps of grass to keep myself from sliding right off the path. Zillah didn't look back, though she must have heard the rattle of stones. It was a long way down.

I came down into the dark, cold back of Zillah's cove. There was no sun here, because of the rocks hanging over us. There was a dank, fishy smell, and weed squelched under my feet, mixed up with plastic bottles, and stones, and bits of tarry rope. I didn't like the feeling of the rocks all around, with their steep, slimy sides keeping out the light. It was like being in prison.

I turned, and saw the boathouse. Zillah was crouching by the padlock, opening it. The boathouse was well above the tide-line, and a shingly track led up to it.

Zillah was wrestling with the key. I crunched up the track and asked, "Is it stuck? D'you want me to try?"

"No." Zillah's hair fell forward over her face, so I couldn't see it, but I knew just how it would look. Tight, angry, pushing everyone away. The playground Zillah, crouched over her book. *Don't come near me.* Why was she like that so much of the time? I stood back, and watched as she jiggled the key in the rusty padlock.

That was when I saw the ring. I don't know why I hadn't noticed it before: it must have been on her finger all the time. It was a heavy, sparkly ring which looked too big for Zillah's middle finger. It caught the light and flashed as she struggled to open the padlock, then all at once the key worked, the padlock clicked, and Zillah opened the boathouse door.

I forgot about the ring as I peered into the gloom. There was a smell of varnish and paint and stored-up air. Zillah's boat was laying there, tilted to one side. It was painted blue. I knew all boats had names, but I couldn't see one.

"What's it called? Your boat?"

"*She.* She's called *Wayfarer.*"

Zillah said it as if she didn't care, but there was love in her voice and in her hand as she reached out to touch the side of the boat.

"She's lovely," I said. Imagine having a boat of your own, like Zillah. *Wayfarer* looked strong and solid. Not a child's boat: a real boat. I put out my hand and touched her.

"Are we going to take her out, then?" Zillah asked.

It was strange, as if she was making it *my* decision, when I didn't know anything about boats. I hesitated.

"Or are you scared?"

"Course I'm not scared!"

"I bet you've never been in a boat before."

"Yes, I have."

I had, too. A rowing-boat with Dad, so long ago all I could remember were his hands on the oars, and a slop of water round my feet. I don't even know where it was. On holiday, I think, a long time ago.

"I'll help you carry it down to the water," I said.

"Carry it!" Zillah laughed at me. "What d'you think it's made of? Paper?"

I'd had enough. "OK. You do it."

"What?"

"You do it. It's your boat, you know everything about it, you sort it out. I mean *her*."

"I didn't mean—"

"Yes you did. I bet if you came to London you

43

wouldn't even know how to find a Tube station. Why'm I supposed to know all about boats, suddenly, just because we've moved down here?"

Zillah looked at me as if she'd never seen me before. Really surprised. Almost shocked. I thought of school. People didn't talk back to Zillah there, they just left her alone.

Zillah cleared her throat. "Um – sorry," she said.

"That's OK."

It seemed a long way from the boathouse to the water. Zillah put rollers under the boat, and we had to keep running round to the back, picking them up, putting them back at the front again and then rolling the boat a bit further down.

"Do you always have to do this?" I asked Zillah, panting.

"I just drag her up on the shingle, most of the time, up above the tide-line. But she's put away for the winter now."

Zillah talked about the boat as if it (she) was a person, and a person she liked much better than she liked anyone else. *Wayfarer* had an outboard engine, she told me, but we wouldn't need it today. We were only going out a little way.

Zillah didn't say anything about life-jackets, and there weren't any inside *Wayfarer*. I thought you always had to wear them in boats, like seatbelts in cars, but I didn't want to sound like a visitor again, so I didn't say anything.

Wayfarer wanted to be in the water, you could tell. As soon as we had her half-in, she began to look alive. She twisted, and Zillah straightened her up so the narrow front end was pointing out towards the entrance of the cove. Another wave came in and slapped *Wayfarer* sideways. Zillah kicked off her boots and threw them into the boat. She took off her socks, rolled up her jeans and waded into the water to hold the boat steady. I was still on the beach, wondering if I ought to take off my trainers, when she shouted impatiently, "Come on, Katie. Get in and I'll give us a shove off."

There wasn't any choice now. I stepped cautiously over the side, into the boat. The back of it was still on the shingle, we were still half on land – I could get out if I wanted –

Zillah was behind the boat, shoving. There was a grind of pebbles, then *Wayfarer* came free, swinging sideways. Zillah shoved again, splashing through the shallow water. She swung one leg over the side as if she was climbing on to a bicycle, then the other. She was in. The boat wobbled violently, and I clutched the sides.

"Sit down," said Zillah. "There, in the stern. Just keep still till I get her out."

She shoved off again with the oar, poling us off the beach into deeper water, then she sat down in the middle of the boat, slipped both oars into place, and began to guide us out. It wasn't rowing as I'd seen it done before. Zillah felt her way delicately, moving one oar, then the other. The rocks were huge now that we were down in the water. They reared up on either side of the boat as Zillah took us out of the cove's narrow entrance. Too close. They looked as if they were reaching out for us. We slid past draggles of seaweed clinging to the rocks, and there was that smell again, of weed and fish. It made me shiver. A cloud of angry gulls flew up and screamed above our heads. I looked back and there was the grey beach, looking small and safe, out of reach.

Then we were through the entrance to the cove. My eyes stung because the light was suddenly so dazzling, and *Wayfarer* rocked as she took the first wave. I realized how sheltered we'd been in Zillah's cove. This was the real sea now, and we were out on it. Zillah was pulling hard on the oars, her face creased with effort.

"We're OK now," she said. "We've gone past the shelf. We're in deep water."

I sat still, in the middle of the boat, as she'd told me. The way Zillah said "in deep water" sounded as if she thought it was a good thing, but I wasn't so sure. Zillah was rowing hard, heading straight out to sea, and every time she pulled on the oars the ring flashed on her hand.

Chapter Seven

When the first wave splashed over *Wayfarer*'s side, I wasn't frightened. The water landed with an icy smack on my knees, and poured into the bottom of the boat. We were quite a way out from land, now. When I looked over my shoulder I could see the top of the cliffs. The water chopped and danced, and *Wayfarer* danced too, tossing on top of the waves. I clutched her wooden sides.

But it was still all right, until Zillah stopped rowing. She'd been rowing hard, and I think she just wanted a rest. I think she was as surprised as I was when *Wayfarer* spun sideways, as soon as she brought the oars up out of the water. All at once the waves were smacking us really hard, side-on, making us rock harder and harder with each buffet of water. A big wave flopped over the side and suddenly my trainers were full of water. *Wayfarer* bucked and shuddered all over. I held on tight to her sides, and wondered if this was normal, or if I should be frightened. Zillah grabbed the oars again, dug into the sea with her right oar, and faced *Wayfarer* into the wind. Then it was all right. Rough, but all right. At least it didn't feel as if the waves were trying to turn *Wayfarer* over, and push us into the sea.

"Don't you think we should go back, Zillah?" I said. "We're a long way out."

"What's the matter? Are you scared?"

"No," I said, and it was true. I wasn't scared, I was angry. Angry with Zillah, and the games she was playing. She lived here. She was supposed to know all about boats, and the sea. *We'll take the boat out for a bit*, she'd told me. But she knew she was going to row straight out to sea. She'd planned it. She *wanted* me to be scared, begging to go back.

I wasn't going to. I was as good a swimmer as Zillah, I was sure. Probably better. I measured the distance to the cliffs and wondered if I could swim it, but I knew I couldn't, not in this cold, wild November water. It wasn't a storm, but it was rough, and if *Wayfarer* didn't like it, I wouldn't be able to swim through it.

Ahead of us a bigger wave rose. I saw the inside of it, green, packed with bubbles, rearing up. Zillah couldn't see it, because she was rowing with her back to it. My mouth opened to warn her, but the wave got there first. It broke on Zillah's back, then hurled its weight of water into *Wayfarer*. I shut my eyes.

"Bail, Katie, while I turn her," yelled Zillah. "*Bail!*"

I opened my eyes. Zillah was soaked, and there were centimetres of water in the bottom of the boat.

"Bail?"

"Plastic can under the seat." She was fighting to stop the sea from taking her oars. "Quick, Katie!"

There was the red plastic can. Scoop up the water and throw it over. I can do that. I scooped and threw, scooped and threw, scooped and threw. Another wave heaved a bucket-load back over the side, but I threw it back. I was going to win. I had something to do now. It was much better than clinging to the side of the boat while Zillah took me wherever she wanted. I was part of it, helping *Wayfarer*.

My can bashed against Zillah's feet as she struggled to turn *Wayfarer*. For a horrible moment we were sideways to the waves again, rocking violently, punched about in the water like a toy boat. Then Zillah got *Wayfarer* round and started to row as hard as she could, back to shore. The wind whipped her hair over her face, and behind her the cliffs rose up, with waves pounding at their base. I hoped she knew the way back. I hoped it wouldn't be too hard to steer *Wayfarer* into that narrow entrance to the cove. But Zillah must have done it loads of times before, I told myself. It couldn't be as dangerous as it looked. Could it?

I kept on bailing. We didn't seem to be sinking but I wasn't taking any chances. As fast as I flung the water out, the sea flung it back at me. *Wayfarer* rode on. Every few minutes Zillah glanced behind her. We'd come quite a way down the coast, as well as out to sea. I couldn't even see the cove any more. *Zillah must know where it is,* I thought. But she was glancing behind her more and more often now, and pulling harder on the oars. Suddenly she stared straight at me, not smiling, not angry, not hiding anything. Almost like a friend.

"We've got into the current," she said.

"What?"

"There's a current here, a strong one. It'll take us south-west unless we can get out of it. Can't you feel it?"

I didn't know what she meant.

"I'm rowing as hard as I can," she said, "but I can't bring us in. I'm going to change direction, try to cut across the current on the diagonal. I can't do it going straight across. The current's too strong."

I didn't really understand. I couldn't feel the muscle of the current pulling against her oars, as she could. But I understood that we were slipping farther and farther from where we should be. We were out in deep water all right.

"It's a bad current," said Zillah. "It'll take us on to the Gurnard Rocks."

She didn't say it as if she wanted to scare me. I don't think she *did* want to scare me any more. She wanted my help.

"She'll take in a lot of water when I turn her. You ready to bail hard?"

I nodded. "Is there another can?"

"Use your trainer."

I tugged off my left trainer. Trainer in one hand, plastic can in the other. I was ready.

"Ready?" said Zillah. "Hold tight. It'll get rough."

It did get rough. As *Wayfarer* battled round to cross the current on the diagonal, the sea hit us again, sideways, drenching, freezing, shovelling heaps of water into the bottom of the boat. I bailed the trainer to the left, the can to the right. Trainer, can. Trainer, can. Trainer, can. I was going to beat that sea. I wasn't going to let it get me. The sea thought it was going to win but it wasn't. Zillah and I were winning. Zillah was grunting with effort like a tennis player on TV, and *Wayfarer* was struggling forward, crossing the current. I could feel it now, the fight between Zillah and the current which wanted to sweep us down the coast and on to the rocks. Trainer to the left, can to the right. Trainer, can. Trainer, can. I hurled the water back into the face of the sea. *Don't think you're going to win, because you're not.* Trainer, can, trainer, can, trainer...

"It's OK," said Zillah. "You can stop now."

I looked down at my feet. There was hardly any water in the boat. I looked up. The cliffs were closer. Zillah was leaning back, resting on her oars. She was shaking with the effort.

"We're out of the current," Zillah said. "I'm going to bring her in a bit more, and then we can start making our way up the coast."

The sea slapped and bubbled round the boat. It hadn't got us this time, but it could wait. *Next time, you might not be so lucky. You'd better show me some respect.*

I patted *Wayfarer*'s side. She'd done her best for us. She hadn't let the sea turn her over, or swamp her. She'd fought her way out of the current. She hadn't let the sea get us.

"She's a good old boat," said Zillah, and she dug the oars into the water again, and began to row us home.

It was then I looked up. I saw something on top of the cliff. A figure, standing still, looking out to sea. But it was too far away to see who it was.

Chapter Eight

Zillah poured water into the pan from a plastic bottle, stirred in powdered milk, and turned up the gas flame under it. We'd both wrapped old blankets round ourselves. Zillah keeps blankets in the boathouse, and a Calor-gas stove, and a tin full of biscuits and chocolates. I was eating a Mars Bar she'd given me, and trying not to shiver. I'd been hot while I was bailing and then helping Zillah haul *Wayfarer* up into the boathouse, but now I could feel my wet jeans clinging to my legs, and the cold squelchy insides of my trainers.

When the milk had boiled, Zillah mixed in chocolate powder, then poured the hot chocolate into two mugs. I cupped my hands round my mug and drank, not caring that the chocolate scalded my mouth. It felt fantastic. The heat of it spread out from my stomach, down my arms and legs. All at once I was so tired I wanted to go to sleep right there on the floor of the boathouse, wrapped up in the blanket. But something caught my eyes. Zillah's ring, shining as she lifted her mug.

"I like your ring," I said.

Zillah frowned. I thought she was going to ignore me, then she said, "It's mine."

"Course it's yours. I didn't say it wasn't. I just said I liked it."

Slowly, reluctantly, the frown left Zillah's face.

"It used to belong to my great-aunt. She left it to me. They're diamonds. They're dirty, they need cleaning. But they're real diamonds."

"Diamonds! Wow! It must be worth loads of money."

"I know it is. But I'm not selling it. And no one else is selling it, either. It belonged to my great-aunt Zillah, and she wanted me to have it, because I always used to play with it when I was little."

Zillah sounded as if she expected someone to come in and snatch the ring any moment. I wondered why. Anyway, she needn't worry. I didn't want her dirty diamonds.

"I wear it all the time," Zillah went on. "Even at school. I put it on a string round my neck, because we aren't allowed to wear jewellery. I wear it at night, too."

This girl was *definitely* worried about burglars.

"I thought it was really safe round here. No burglars or anything. That's what Mum said."

Zillah hesitated. Then she burst out: "It's not burglars. It's Dad."

"Your dad?"

"Yeah," said Zillah sullenly. "He reckons I ought to sell it. Reckons the farm ought to have the money. But that's not what Great-aunt Zillah wanted. She told me *I* was going to have it.

"She put it in her will, too. It's there in black and white, whatever Dad says. She left me the cottage as well. The cottage where you're living. *To my great-niece and namesake, Zillah, in loving remembrance.*"

"Oh. I see," I said faintly. "When did she die?"

"Two years ago. But she didn't just *die*. She was murdered."

"Murdered!" I was sure Zillah was joking. It couldn't be true.

"She was." Zillah hunched up her knees. "And I know who did it."

"Do you? Who?"

Zillah scowled at me, but I didn't think she meant it. It was just a habit. Zillah scowls too much, and I smile too much, even when I don't feel like smiling at all. I wanted to ask loads of questions about Great-aunt Zillah and who the murderer was, and how they'd done it. But I didn't ask anything. Already, I felt as if I knew Zillah much better than I'd done that morning, when she came creeping into our kitchen. We'd had to fight to get the boat back, and we'd done it together. We'd both been frightened, even though Zillah wouldn't show it. It was something we would never, ever be able to tell our families. I knew I'd never forget bailing with my trainer and the can while Zillah rowed across the current, not if I lived to be as old as Great-aunt Zillah. Zillah wasn't my enemy any more, if she ever had been.

Zillah sighed deeply. Then she said, "You know all those TV programmes where people get murdered?"

"Yes."

"It's always a stranger, isn't it? Then they get caught and put in prison and no one has to think about them any more."

I didn't understand what she meant, but I said yes again. There was another silence.

"But what if the murderer's someone you know," said Zillah at last. "Someone who's part of your family."

I thought of Angry Janice straight away. I could imagine her shouting. I could imagine her throwing things, or maybe even slapping Zillah, if she got angry enough. But surely not murdering someone...

"You mean your mum?" I suggested, very cautiously. Zillah looked amazed.

"My mum?"

"Umm ... yeah ... what you were talking about, Zillah." I cleared my throat. It was so hard to say it out loud. "Um … murdering your great-aunt, I mean." It sounded so stupid.

"Not my *mum*," said Zillah, as if I was a complete idiot. "My dad."

"Your dad," I repeated. "Oh. I see."

I didn't see anything. It wasn't Angry Janice then, but Geoff. Geoff the Murderer. It couldn't be true. Old ladies don't get murdered by their nephews, in cottages in Cornwall. I mean, the police would have come. Wouldn't they? But Zillah was silent. She was still scowling, but this time it was the kind of scowling you do when you're trying not to cry.

The hundreds of questions I still wanted to ask died in my throat. It *couldn't* be true, I told myself again.

"Don't you dare tell anyone," said Zillah fiercely. "I'll know if you do."

"I won't."

"No one knows about it. Only me."

But she'd told me. Maybe she felt the same as I did. As if we were in this together.

"You want some more hot chocolate? There's plenty in the pan."

I dragged my mind away from dirty diamonds and dead great-aunts. There was too much to think about. And I was too tired, and too cold. Even with the blanket around me, and the hot chocolate inside me, I couldn't stop shivering. I wanted to get home, to Mum. It must be late. It must be nearly dinner-time –

"Oh no!"

"What?"

"Your dad's supposed to be taking us into St Ives. You know Mum's van's broken down. We can't get it fixed until she's got enough money for a new car-burettor. We're supposed to meet your dad at twelve-thirty."

"Well, you've missed him, then," said Zillah. "But you haven't missed much."

Zillah certainly seemed to hate her dad. But it wasn't surprising, if she thought he'd really –

But it couldn't be true. After all, you don't have murderers living just up the lane from you, do you?

Chapter Nine

I was going to creep through the kitchen, up the stairs, dump Zillah's blanket, change my clothes. Mum would never know what had happened.

It didn't work out like that. As I came up the path, the door flew open. Mum rushed out, grabbed me, and hugged me so tight it hurt. Then she burst into tears.

"Katie! Where have you been? I've been so worried. I've been up to the farm, and down the coast path looking for you. I even climbed down to the beach. I didn't know where you'd gone."

She was shaking. I felt terrible, as if I'd done it on purpose.

"What time is it, Mum?"

"It's half-past two! You *knew* we were going out at half-past twelve. And what are you doing wrapped up in that blanket? What's happened?"

"It's nothing, Mum. I just got a bit wet. Zillah gave me the blanket."

"You fell off the cliff! I know you did!"

"Mum, if I'd fallen off the cliff I'd be dead. I just slipped on the beach and got a bit wet, that's all."

In my experience a good, solid lie which bears no resemblance to the truth always works better than a half-truth. Above all, I knew I mustn't let the word "boat" slip out. Mum would be on to it at once. She'd stopped crying, and she was pulling off the blanket and feeling my wet jeans and jacket.

"Quick, let's get you inside and into some dry clothes. You'll freeze to death out here."

I followed her into the cottage, trailing the blanket after me. Mum was so upset, it was as if she knew everything that had happened. The waves nearly swamping the boat, the current that might have taken us on to the rocks, me bailing and Zillah rowing for safety. But she couldn't possibly know any of it. As far as Mum knew, I was just late, that was all. And she was always telling me how safe it was here in the country, with no lorries thundering by or strange men lurking in parks.

Mum followed me upstairs and started dragging clean clothes out of my drawers, and fetching towels. I would have given a million pounds for ten minutes in our power-shower, with hot water streaming down all over me, and a hot towel from the radiator afterwards.

"I know!" said Mum. "I'll make you a mustard bath. It'll stop you getting a cold. Come on down as soon as you're ready, Katie, but don't put your socks on."

It took me a while to get changed. My fingers were so cold that they fumbled with everything. I was tired, and a bit shaky, and in a way I longed to go downstairs to Mum and cuddle up to her and tell her everything. Except that I knew she would never ever let me go anywhere again with Zillah, if I did. And, amazingly enough, I still wanted to. I could even imagine going out in *Wayfarer* again with Zillah, down the coast, in and out of the little coves. I didn't think she'd try to scare me again. She'd been pretty scared herself. Zillah might think she was tough, but the sea was a lot tougher.

When I came down, Mum was pouring some powder into a bowl of steaming hot water.

"Sit down on this chair and put your feet in here," she commanded.

"I'm not putting my feet in mustard, Mum. I'm not a sausage."

"It's a *mustard bath*, Katie. Put your feet in here NOW."

Mum rarely shouts at me, and when she does I rarely argue. I lowered my feet gingerly into the steaming-hot water.

"Ow! Mum, it's boiling!"

"It won't kill you," said Mum. "Sit like that for ten minutes and you'll warm up."

I had to admit that the mustard bath smelled quite nice. And it was true, I was beginning to feel much warmer. The heat flowed up through me, tingling. Mum knelt down and carefully poured some more hot water into the bowl. Then she looked up at me, and smiled. "Feeling better?"

"Yes, loads. Mum, what happened about Zillah's dad?"

"He wasn't too pleased. Never mind, we can always go to St Ives another day. The main thing is that you're all right. Do you know, Katie, I got so frightened –"

She said it just as if she was talking to an adult friend, like Bridget.

"I was all right."

"Yes, I know. But I suppose I worry more now... You know, I was walking on the path, along the cliff, and I stopped to sketch. There was a little boat way out to sea. I started sketching it – the light was wonderful, with the boat bouncing up and down on the waves. All that sea and sky and light and a tiny boat in the middle of it. But suddenly I had the strangest feeling. I felt so frightened – panicky, almost. I didn't know where you were. I felt so afraid. Stupid, wasn't it? All because of a little boat."

Mum was looking up at me intently, staring deep into my face. But I knew it wasn't because she suspected that I'd been in that boat. She was trying to tell me something quite different, and I wasn't sure what it was.

"I suppose it's because of Dad," Mum said. "I never used to get frightened about you."

"You did. You were always on about traffic and strangers, when we were in London."

"Maybe." She smiled. "I'll show you my sketches later."

"Mum."

"What?"

"Don't be frightened. I'm fine."

"I know. Especially now you've had that mustard bath."

"Can I take my feet out yet?"

Mum showed me her sketches later. They were good: too good. She had captured the shining curve of the sea, and the waves, and the wildness of the light. There was the boat in the middle of it, a frail, black speck with two tiny figures, so far away you couldn't tell if they were men or women. Or children. It gave me the strangest feeling as I stared at the paper and knew Mum had drawn us, not knowing who we were. Me and Zillah, almost lost, miles out on the wilderness of the sea. Surely we hadn't gone that far? In Mum's drawing, it didn't look as if we'd ever get back.

"It's good for me, being here," said Mum

thoughtfully. "It's good for my work." She continued to stare at the paper. I knew she was thinking of the painting she would build up from that sketch, hour after hour in her studio. I knew she was as far away from me in her mind as that boat was from the land.

Suddenly there was a tap on the door. Mum jumped. "I wonder who that can be?"

It was only about half-past four, but it was already getting dark. The clouds had come down and the wind was rising.

"I'll open it," I said.

"No, you stay by the stove."

Mum opened the door. "Oh, Zillah, hello. Have you come to see Katie?"

"Mm, yeah, just called in," mumbled Zillah. "I won't stay."

"Come on in. Katie's keeping warm by the stove. She got soaked through, mucking about on the beach."

Relief flashed across Zillah's face. "You all right, then, Katie?" she asked.

"Fine. Mum was just showing me some of the drawings she did today," I added maliciously. I felt it would do Zillah good to have a surprise for a change.

"They're only sketches," said Mum. "I've got a lot of work to do ... but I think I may have got the basis for something..."

Zillah bent over the table. Then she went very still.

"Why, that's –" she said, then she stopped herself. "That's good."

"It's just marks at this stage," said Mum. "Notes to myself. But all the same, there's something – the light, and all that water – and then the boat with the two little figures. I can do something with it."

Zillah said nothing. Her look rested on Mum, then on me.

"It's nice in here," she said at last. "You've made it nice."

I tried to see the kitchen through Zillah's eyes. Mum had the stove door open so the warm light of it spilled into the room. There was Mum's favourite terracotta cloth on the table, and a heap of oranges in a dark yellow bowl one of her friends had made. On the wall there was a painting Mum did years ago, of an old man in a pub in Dublin, drinking Guinness. And on the floor there was the bowl full of mustard bath, which we hadn't got round to throwing away yet.

"Stay and have some tea, Zillah," Mum said.

Zillah's face closed over. "No," she said. "I've got to go. See you, Katie."

When she'd gone Mum fetched some apples to bake, along with the potatoes which she'd put in earlier. I cut out the cores with a paring knife, and stuffed them with brown sugar. Mum said she'd go up to the farm to get some cream.

"Saturday night treat," she said.

"Saturday night! That means we've been here a whole week."

But it feels much longer. It feels as if we've crossed the border, and we're really living here now. The cottage, Janice, the outside toilet, school, Susie, the noise of the wind, the fires in my bedroom, *Wayfarer,* Mum's studio, the smell of baking apples, Zillah's ring...

We're not visitors any more.

Chapter Ten

If we had a phone, I'd call Jessie now. After a day like today, I need to talk to someone.

1) I was late for the bus. Everyone yelled as I ran up to the stop, "Come on KATIE, come on KATIE." Then my bag burst open and my school library book fell into the mud. I grabbed it and collapsed up the steps of the bus and into the nearest seat.

Susie was offended because I hadn't sat by her. "I suppose you think you don't need me any more, now you've been here a whole week," she sniffed.

"It's not like that, Susie. I was just getting my stuff together." So she relented and I had to sit with her anyway, and listen to very boring stories about the Guides' disco she'd gone to on Saturday night. *All the way to school.* (Zillah was locked into a book as usual, not looking at anyone.)

2) I'd completely forgotten to do my homework.

3) Mr Trevelyan was in a terrible mood anyway, because a fox got his organic chickens.

4) Nick Hart asked me if my parents were divorced, because I'm living on my own with my mum.

5) Susie did tricks with her new bionic yo-yo *all dinner-time* without giving anyone else a go.

6) Zillah read, and read, and read.

7) I looked around the playground and realized there wasn't anyone in the whole of Cornwall I'd known for longer than nine days.

8) It started pouring with rain again after dinner-time.

However, things began to improve after that. Mr Trevelyan asked if I'd go and give a message to his wife about some new chickens he'd ordered on the Internet. He'd downloaded two pages of information, and printed it out for her. So I ran and knocked on the Trevelyans' door, and Mrs T came out looking harassed, but quite friendly. She has lots of brown hair which she pins up on top of her head, but it keeps falling down. The baby was tucked under her arm, screeching, and the other two were racing their trikes round and round the sitting-room. They kept bashing into things, but that didn't matter, because there was almost no furniture. Mrs T said they were upset about the chickens, which had been found scattered round the garden when they went out to play. "*No heads*," mouthed Mrs T. But the middle one heard, anyway, and started bawling and screaming.

"Oh God," said Mrs T. "Katie, could you be an absolute angel and read them a story? I've *got* to change this baby. Wee is practically *cascading* down his legs."

Mrs T is terribly posh. She sounds as if she ought to be tearing round London in a Land Rover, not picking up headless chickens in a Cornwall garden.

"*Don't ever think* that just one more baby won't make much difference," she said darkly, as she left the room.

I was alone with two little kids. The middle one had stopped screaming, and was staring at me with his thumb stuck in his mouth. Then he took the thumb out and said, "Story."

"Sweetie," said the other one. I grabbed a book from a pile in the corner before they could think of anything else they wanted.

"Not that one. We want *Mr Magnolia*."

"*Mr Magnolia*. Right." I flicked through the pile of books. Most of them had been chewed, and some had lumps of old food stuck to the covers.

"Only one boot," said the middle one. Finally I found the right book. Half the cover was torn off, but they didn't care. I sat down on the sofa and they jammed themselves in close to me, breathing heavily, a bit like the cows in the lane. When I started reading, I remembered the story. It was one Dad used to read to me when I was little. We used to yell out the chorus together, as loud as we could. MR MAGNOLIA HAS ONLY ONE BOOT!

Mr Trevelyan's kids were pretty good at yelling, too. I didn't notice that Mrs T had come back into the room, without the baby.

"He's fallen asleep, thank God," she said. "You two can watch your Teletubbies video."

Mrs T settled them on cushions in front of the TV, and flopped down on the sofa, shutting her eyes. I thought she might be going to sleep, then she said, without opening her eyes, "Chickens. Is that what it's about?"

"Yes, it's about some new ones Sir's ordered from the Internet. He wants you to look at all the stuff about them."

"Oh God. Leave it on the table. I mean, it was pretty horrible about the F-O-X, but I can't say I'm frightfully sorry they've gone. The noise ... and the SMELL. Cleaning them out – and treating all their disgusting diseases – and stopping the children trying to put them in their dolls' prams –"

I knew I should get back to the classroom, but I didn't want to. It was great being with Mrs T. You could tell she always said exactly what she thought.

"I'll stagger up and make us some coffee in a moment. I just don't seem to be able to keep my eyes open."

"I could make the coffee," I suggested.

"You're an angel. And there's one C-H-O-C-O-L-A-T-E B-I-S-C-U-I-T in the tin on top of the fridge. You have it. Don't let *them* see it, or there'll be absolute hell to pay."

I could imagine this. I ate the C-H-O-C-O-L-A-T-E B-I-S-C-U-I-T in record time, and made two mugs of coffee.

"Wonderful. You're living in Zillah's cottage, aren't you?"

"Yes." I wondered how Mrs T knew that Zillah had inherited the cottage.

"She was fabulous. I used to take Josh down there a lot when he was a baby."

I realized she wasn't talking about my Zillah, but about old Great-aunt Zillah, the one who'd died two years ago.

"She was extraordinary," said Mrs T thoughtfully. "She did everything for herself, kept a small-holding until she was seventy, went for a five-mile walk every day, whatever the weather. Little Zillah used to be down there at the cottage the whole time. She adored her great-aunt. I hope I'm like that when I'm old, but somehow I don't think there's much chance. These three will have finished me off long before that. Do you know, Katie, I used to think I was really *quite a nice person*. Now I'm like a fish-wife by seven-thirty in the morning. Because they absolutely *don't sleep*, you know. This is what people never tell you."

"What did she die of? Great-aunt Zillah?" I asked.

Mrs T's face changed. "She had a bad time, poor darling," she said. "She had a stroke and she couldn't move the right-hand side of her body. You could tell she just wanted to die. It was awful. She couldn't walk, she couldn't go out in the garden, or feed the goats. She hated it. And she couldn't speak properly. The only one who could always understand her was little Zillah. Oh no, the video's finished."

The room disintegrated. I grabbed my mug off the floor as the kids jumped on their trikes and began to zoom around again. Mrs T started yelling at them to be quiet and not wake the baby. It was time to go.

"Tell Richard the chicken stuff was terrific," said Mrs T, "and it took us ages to read through it, didn't it, Katie?" She gave me a big, wicked grin. "Make sure you come again. I can't tell you how I long for some civilized company."

Rain was still driving down as she opened the door.

"It's funny, talking about Zillah. It made me see her so clearly... I do miss her. Poor little Zillah, she never got over it."

Chapter Eleven

I got soaking wet running home from the school bus stop. Zillah ran with me as far as the farm. The weather was worse than ever. Even Zillah would have to admit that it was a real storm this time. The wind had got underneath the black plastic that covers the rolls of silage (that's something cows eat, don't ask me what). It had ripped one cover in half and another was starting to tear. Zillah and I tried to fix it down with heavy stones, but they just rolled off.

"I'll get my dad," Zillah said. It was the first time I'd heard her talk about him as if he was a normal dad, not Geoff the Murderer. When we got to the barn we had to flatten ourselves against the wall because the wind wouldn't let us round the corner. It was just like being in a film where the baddies are waiting round the side of the building. Zillah grabbed me and pulled me into the shelter of the barn doorway.

"You want to come in for a bit?" she asked.

I hesitated. I *did* want to, but after Mum getting so frightened when I was late back last time, I thought I'd better get home straight away. Mum knows what time the school bus gets in.

"Sorry, Zillah," I said. "I would if I could phone Mum. But I don't want her to get worried..."

I thought Zillah would scowl as usual, but she didn't. A bit awkwardly, she said, "You could ask your mum if you can come tomorrow."

"Yes, that'd be great. I'll ask her."

I said goodbye and splashed off down the lane to the cottage. Yeah, it would be great to go to Zillah's house, and have tea with Geoff the Murderer, Angry Janice and Scowling Zillah. But on the other hand, it was beginning to look as if Zillah did want to be friends.

As soon as I got home, Mum started worrying about getting me some proper waterproofs, and a pair of boots that could cope with all the winter mud. Amazingly enough, she seems to think that the weather will get *even worse*. And then I opened my backpack and found that it wasn't waterproof, as I'd thought. All the ink had run on the computer sheets of maths I was supposed to be doing for homework. I couldn't read any of it. Mr Trevelyan was going to go completely mad if I went in for the second day and said I hadn't done my homework.

"I'll write you a note," said Mum.

She really doesn't understand about how teachers look when they open that kind of note.

"Hmmm. Your mum says you couldn't do your homework because it got *rained on*, Katie. *Good try*. At least you've got an original excuse. See me later for double homework tonight."

"We'll just have to get you a really good back-pack," said Mum. But I knew it wasn't as easy as that. Mum isn't making much money. Usually she does quite a lot of children's book illustration, but she's concentrating on her weather studies now. Even when the paintings are finished, it'll take ages before she sells them and gets any money.

People think we must have lots of money, because Dad died in an accident. But he didn't have any life insurance. It wasn't his fault. He was only thirty-seven. No one thinks they are going to die when they are thirty-seven. Anyway, we're really lucky, because we've got people living in our house in London who pay us rent. Mum says the rent just about pays the mortgage. She talks to me about all this kind of stuff now, because there's only Mum and me. It's good, really, because I understand things better. I don't ask for things we can't afford. (At least, most of the time I don't.) But it would be fantastic if Mum sold her paintings. We might even get a car, instead of a broken-down van.

Mum is working in her studio now. I'm in my

room, curled up on the rug in front of the fire. I haven't got my light on, because I love the way all the rosy shadows stretch out and jump on the white walls. When you've got a fire you don't have to do anything, you just watch it. Which is just as well, as the TV reception is so terrible tonight that *Neighbours* looked as if it was taking place in a snowstorm. I told Mum I'd wash up, and I will in a minute. I've just finished writing a letter to Jessie. Half-writing a letter, really. I started telling her all about the boat and Zillah and then I realized how crazy and dangerous it all sounded. If Jessie's mum ever read the letter she would probably come zooming straight down to Cornwall to tell my mum I was At Risk. (Jessie's mum is a social worker.) Anyway, it's useless writing to people when you really want to talk to them. But Mum says Jessie can come down and stay with us in the Christmas holidays. I hope she'll like it here. It would be awful if she hated it, and I found out she was just waiting to go home. I can't really imagine Jessie stomping up the lane in the mud and cow-pats. But then, a few weeks ago I wouldn't have been able to imagine me going to the outside toilet *at night*, on my own, with only a torch to frighten away the spiders...

I wonder if this was Great-aunt Zillah's bedroom? Mum gave me the bigger bedroom, because she's got the studio as well. I think if I were Great-aunt

Zillah, I'd have chosen this room. It looks over the garden, and down to the sea. And it's got a nice feeling. You know how some rooms have, and some rooms haven't? You can tell as soon as you walk into them.

Mum says this cottage is really old. Maybe more than three hundred years old. Think of all the people who've lived here and watched the firelight on the walls, just like me. And all the talking that's gone on in here, and the laughing. I bet Zillah used to sit here, with her great-aunt. Mrs T said she was always down at the cottage.

Mum's calling – better go. I've got to ask her about going to tea with Geoff the Murderer. Zillah was stupid, really, telling me that, and then asking me to go there for tea. She must know I'll find out it isn't true. It *can't* be true.

But Zillah *has* got the diamond ring. And she does wear it all the time. It was round her neck at school, today, on a string. I saw it when we changed for PE.

Mum showed me her new work. She's making sketches for a painting of the wind. Of course you can't paint the wind, but you paint it through showing what it does. Or at least, that's what Mum said. She showed me a thick pile of sketches: twisted trees, cows sheltering by the side of the granite hedge, the long grass being combed flat, little figures bowed down, battling against the wind, their clothes plastered against their bodies. Just like me and Zillah when we came round the side of the barn. The sketch I liked best was one of a man on a bike, hunched over the handlebars, struggling uphill. You could almost hear the wind buffeting him.

"I want to do a huge landscape," Mum said. "A really big painting." Her eyes shone with excitement. "This place is wonderful for my work, Katie. It's like a new world."

Certainly is, I thought. I turned the drawings over and looked at them again. They were frightening, in a way. Everything was moving and nothing was certain. Even the people looked as if they could be blown off the face of the earth any moment. Mum never used to want to do huge paintings. She never drew like this in London.

London is a dangerous word. When I think of it, it's like opening a door and there's our old life, still going on. Except that I can't touch it.

After Dad died, Mum didn't go into her studio for a long time. As soon as I left for school she went out. Sometimes she went to see Bridget in her studio, or another of her friends. Sometimes she just walked. I think she walked all day. One day she told me she'd walked all the way to Hampstead Heath, which is miles from our house. She started picking me up from school, which she hadn't done for ages. When we got home, the cereal bowls and Mum's coffee cup would still be on the kitchen table. No fire on in the studio, no radio playing, no pile of used coffee cups, no smell of paint and turps, no Mum lost in her work, with paint on her forehead where she'd pushed her hair back.

Before Dad died we were a family, then suddenly we weren't one any more. Just me and Mum, each of us trying to pretend to be OK.

As soon as I got in from school, I used to switch the TV on loud. I turned on all the lights, and I talked loads to Mum, so that the house felt a bit like it used to do. Dad never cared how much noise I made. Mum said it was always Dad who calmed me down when I was a screaming baby. He used to dance round the room with me in the sling. He loved music, and cars revving, and people yelling from room to room, and phones ringing all the time, and friends calling round. If someone in our street had a party and the noise went booming on until about two in the morning, Dad was happy. Usually he was at the party anyway.

Dad never went to bed early, and he didn't really care if I did or not. Most of the time I did, because Mum made me, but if she was out for the evening I always stayed up with Dad, playing cards or watching old videos or looking at Dad's collection of maps and atlases and planning where we wanted to travel.

I don't think we ever looked at a map of Cornwall. What would Dad think if he could see us here now?

Chapter Twelve

I didn't get into trouble about the homework. Mr Trevelyan was so excited about our new on-line link to a school in Yakutsk that he actually smiled after he had read Mum's note, and gave me a plastic folder to put my worksheets in.

"That'll keep the rain off," he said. "Oh no, time for Assembly already. Why is it always time for Assembly when I'm in the middle of something interesting?" He gazed longingly at the computer.

"Come on, Sir," said Mark firmly. "Mrs Isaacs has sent a message to say the little ones are all in the Hall waiting. I'll put the computers on sleep mode, shall I?"

School here is completely different from London. There were more than five hundred kids in my school there. I knew everyone in my year, but you couldn't possibly know all the little ones. Here, you do. Everybody knows everything about everybody else. Lots of families have been living next-door to each other since about the nineteenth century. At first I wondered why the same surnames kept coming up, then Mark explained how all the families round here have been marrying each other for hundreds of years, so loads of children in my school are cousins. Even people you wouldn't think could possibly be related, like Zillah and Susie. People who actually hate each other!

At break today Susie said, "You don't want to waste your time on Zillah Treliske." (This was because Zillah was reading as usual, and I'd asked her if it was a good book. She didn't exactly answer, but she didn't scowl either. I'm sure if Susie hadn't been there, she would have answered.)

"Why?" I asked.

Susie shrugged. "They don't make friends," she said.

"Who don't?"

"The Treliskes. Never have done."

I thought of Great-aunt Zillah, and the way Mrs T had said *I do miss her*, and talked about taking baby Josh down to Great-aunt Zillah's cottage. I didn't believe Susie. I didn't say anything, but Susie must have seen the not-believing in my face.

"*I* should know," she said. "We're cousins."

"What? You and Zillah are cousins?"

Susie nodded.

"But you don't even speak to her," I said.

"No," said Susie. "We haven't spoken for…" she counted it up on her fingers, "…fifty-five years."

"Fifty-five years! You haven't even been alive for fifty-five years, Susie."

"It's not just me, it's all the Buryans," said Susie. She sounded pleased about it, as if a quarrel that went on for fifty-five years made her really important. "Not since my grandad came back from the war and found that Zillah's great-aunt wouldn't marry him. She was going to marry someone else."

"Well, why shouldn't she, if she wanted to?"

"She'd promised. She'd got his ring and everything."

His ring! Maybe that was the one Zillah had around her neck?

"What kind of ring was it?" I asked.

Susie looked at me. "How should I know? Anyway, it doesn't matter, does it. The point is, she married his *brother*. My great-uncle. That's how Zillah's my cousin. And none of the Buryans ever spoke to him again. Or *her*."

"And so you don't speak to Zillah." I wanted to be sure I'd got this right.

"No. Not really. I mean, I'll say things if I have to."

It all sounded really depressing. I couldn't help feeling sorry for Zillah. Susie sounded so sure of herself, so sure that she was right.

"So really…" she said, and then she stopped.

"What?"

"Well, you can be Zillah's friend if you want. Even though she's weird. But I can't really be friends with you if you're going to be friends with her."

Susie stared into my face. She's very pretty, but when she looks like that she's not pretty at all, even with her blue eyes and her curly brown hair bouncing round her cheeks.

"Oh," I mumbled. "Umm, right." I wanted to get away and think about all this without Susie's eyes boring into me. She'd been really nice to me since I'd arrived ... in a way...

I was saved by the bell. Mr Trevelyan came rushing round the playground, clanging it so hard his baby began to cry in the next-door garden. Mrs T zoomed out of the back door.

"Richard, I've asked you about a million times not to ring that bloody bell so loudly!"

We were all looking at one another and grinning, even Susie and Zillah. Suddenly it didn't feel a bit like school.

Chapter Thirteen

I'll tell you about my first sight of Geoff the Murderer. (But I feel mean calling him that, now that I know him.) OK, then: Zillah's dad.

He was climbing a ladder that was propped against the side of the barn. I froze. I couldn't move, I couldn't say anything.

"Come on," said Zillah, running ahead to the house.

When I didn't come after her, she looked back. "Katie, what's wrong?"

"Nothing," I said. "It was just –"

Now that I looked at him properly, Zillah's dad wasn't at all like my dad. He was clambering slowly and carefully up the ladder, with a black plastic sack over his shoulders to keep off the rain.

"Going up for a look at that roof, Zill!" he called across, as if he hoped Zillah would be interested. She didn't answer.

"Let's get in the house," she said. Her dad looked after us, with the rain streaming off his shoulders.

He looked shy and sad and not like Geoff the Murderer at all.

Janice was in the kitchen, angry but pretending not to be because I was there.

"Oh, there you are, Zillah! And Katie, how nice," she said, slamming plates down on to the kitchen table in a way that didn't suggest it was particularly nice at all. "Have you seen your father?"

"Yeah," said Zillah. "He was going up on the barn roof."

Janice slumped into a chair, seized hold of her mug of tea and drank about half of it with her eyes shut.

"Did he say anything?" she asked.

"No," said Zillah.

We were busy for a while, taking off our wet stuff and having a hot drink. Janice was trying to be really friendly, but I felt as if I shouldn't be there. She was so worried, and trying to hide it. Then the back door banged again. It was Zillah's dad. He took off his boots, and walked heavily over to Janice, and stood by her chair. I couldn't help noticing his socks, which were thick, lumpy, hand-knitted ones. I wondered if Janice had made them. He didn't seem to notice me at all, or Zillah. Only Janice, looking at him over her mug of tea.

"We can't get away with it any longer," he said, looking at her desperately. Janice looked horrified. I couldn't believe what I was hearing. Was he going to confess to the murder, right now, in front of us all? And why did he say "we"?

"No," Geoff went on. "We're going to have to have a new roof. That old barn just won't take it any more. That last gale's done for it. And from what I could see up there, it's got to be done right away."

"Oh, no," said Janice. "Can't we do it ourselves? Patch it up again, somehow? Get one of the lads down from Trenwith to give you a hand?"

"No," said Geoff, sitting down heavily opposite her. "We're going to have to face it, girl."

They both looked *so unhappy*. I wished I hadn't come.

"Can I see your room, Zillah?" I asked quickly. Janice seemed to wake up and remember that we were there.

"I'll call you down for tea, girls," she said, in a flat, miserable voice.

We escaped.

Zillah's bedroom was horrible. It was cold, and very tidy. The covers were pulled tight over the bed, and there wasn't much else in the room except a huge black wardrobe which looked a perfect place for a burglar to hide all day and then jump out at you when it got dark. Everything was clean and sad and defeated, like Zillah's dad. The walls were a dingy grey that might have been blue a long time ago, and the window looked out on to black, streaming darkness. There was a smell of damp. I shivered.

But I hadn't noticed the bookcase. It was behind the door as you came in, or I'd have seen it straight away. It was beautiful, the only beautiful thing I'd seen in Zillah's house so far. It was made of smooth, golden wood that shone softly, as if it had a life of its own and it remembered the tree it came from. The top of the bookcase was carved into a pattern of leaves and flowers. Zillah's books were ranged in rows, very neatly. I watched as Zillah knelt down and carefully put the book she'd taken to school back into its place.

"What a lovely bookcase," I said. "Where did you get it?"

I half-thought Great-aunt Zillah might have given it to her. It would be a perfect present, if you loved someone who loved books. Zillah hunched over her shelves. I thought she wasn't going to answer, then she said slowly, reluctantly, "My dad made it for me."

"Your dad made it for you! But it's beautiful."

Then I realized what a stupid thing that was to say. Either it sounded like: *Your dad can't have made it, because it's so good,* or, even worse: *Your dad wouldn't have bothered to make you a bookcase like that, because he doesn't care about you.*

Zillah's dad must have spent hours and hours making it. Each flower and leaf was so beautifully carved, and every edge was smoothed and rounded. There were different-sized shelves for different-sized books. You couldn't make something like that for someone, unless you cared about them.

"You've got so many books," I said. "It's nearly full."

"Yeah, I know. But I don't reckon Dad'll be making me another one like this."

"No one could make another one like this. I bet it's unique."

Zillah smiled. She ran her finger along the wood, stroking it.

"My dad," I said, "my dad was no good at stuff like this."

Zillah shot me a quick look. I knew she knew about Dad being dead, but we'd never said anything about it.

"Wasn't he?"

"No. Useless."

We didn't say anything else for a bit, then Zillah showed me some of her books, and I told her about what I liked reading. I was holding one of her books, and looking at the illustrations, when she suddenly said, "Katie, your hands are shaking."

They were, and I knew why. "It's just that I'm cold, Zillah. Do you think we could light a fire?"

"A fire?" said Zillah, as if she'd never heard of heating a bedroom.

"Yes. You've got a fireplace."

"I've never had a fire in it. I think the chimney's blocked."

"Oh."

"You could borrow one of my jumpers. Mum knits them for me."

She opened the wardrobe and hauled out a huge jumper which was exactly the colour of old cabbage. It came down to my knees when I put it on. Zillah looked at me thoughtfully.

"That should keep you warm."

"Mmm."

The door of the wardrobe swung open and I caught sight of myself in the long spotty mirror.

"Oh my God."

"You can see why I don't wear it to school," said Zillah.

"Mmm."

But at least it was warm. My brain began to work again, and I had a great idea.

"Zillah. We could paint your room. It wouldn't take long, if we both worked on it. If you chose the right colour, you could make the whole room look a lot warmer. You shouldn't have blue facing north – this is north-facing, isn't it?"

I could hear myself getting going. Mum calls it

"Katie the interior decorator", but who cares? Zillah's room looked so horrible that anything we did would be an improvement.

"Yellow, maybe. Or a pale apricot," I suggested. I was beginning to see how it could be. Zillah stared at me.

"It would be difficult to do it," she said at last. "Wouldn't it?"

I knew I'd been right. Zillah didn't really want a freezing cold, dingy bedroom. She just didn't believe that there was any choice. If your walls were grey, that was what you were stuck with.

"It's easy," I said. "We can do all the work. And Mum would let you have the white gloss that's left over from doing the studio, for the door and the windows. Mum could take us to get the paint for the walls, as well – she always finds bargains."

Zillah was thinking. "I could ask Mum..." Then her face closed over. "It's no good. All they'll be thinking about is how to pay for the barn roof. And Dad'll start going on and on to me again about how I could sell my ring. And Great-aunt Zillah –"

"I know," I said quickly. She was getting really upset, in a Zillah-ish, scowling way. "I'll think of another way. Maybe we could earn some money."

Zillah turned back to her bookcase, and began to choose a book for the next day.

"Zillah," I asked, "when did your dad make the bookcase?"

"In the summer, two years ago. Just before Great-aunt Zillah died. Just before he killed her."

She said it in a low voice, not angry or sad, just completely sure. But it couldn't be true. Other people would have known. You can't just kill someone and get away with it. The more I'd thought about it since Zillah first told me in the boathouse, the more I'd been sure she must have got it wrong.

It was as if Zillah could see what I was thinking. "You think I'm lying, don't you?" she said ferociously. "You think things like that don't happen in real life. Well, they do. He gave her some tablets mixed up in a drink. All her tablets."

"But, Zillah, how do you know? I thought she had a stroke."

"I know she had a stroke, but she was all right. She was getting better, I know she was."

"People do die of strokes."

"He crushed up the tablets and gave them to her. I was watching through the door. Then he said, 'Here you are, this'll help you sleep better.' I thought he was helping her. And then the next day she was dead."

The way Zillah said it, it sounded completely true. And she'd been there. She'd seen it. I didn't know what to say. The room felt colder than ever, even though I was wearing the jumper.

"Zillah! Katie! Come on down."

Janice was an expert at pretending. You could tell from her face that she'd been crying, but she kept on chatting about this and that and asking me if I wanted more bread or another piece of cake. The cake was fabulous, so I had three pieces and she looked pleased. Geoff (the Murderer?) sat in a heap at the other end of the table, crumbling up cake. Once or twice he glanced at Zillah as if he wanted to say something to her. The ring shone on Zillah's finger. *Diamonds,* I thought. Enough money to buy a new roof, maybe. Definitely enough money to buy a pot of paint, and unblock a chimney. But the ring was Zillah's, and it was her choice.

"Katie reckons," said Zillah, suddenly, in a loud, challenging voice, "that I could paint my room."

"Paint your room! Of course you can have your room painted," said Janice, much too eagerly. "You know how long I've been wanting to get my hands on that room of yours. I feel ashamed to let anyone go into it, the way it is. What must Katie think!"

"I don't want you to get your hands on my room," said Zillah. "I want to do it myself. With Katie."

Amazingly enough, her mother didn't even tell her off, let alone go into outer space, as Mum would have done if I'd spoken to her like that. Janice just flushed slowly, and looked down. After a minute she said. "It's your room, Zillah. You can do what you want in there."

"Do what I want!" shouted Zillah, scraping back her chair and standing up. "You never, ever think about what I want! You don't care about me at all. All you think about is the barn roof. Farm, farm, farm, that's all you care about. Not me."

Her father raised his head. He started to speak, slowly, as if it was hard for him to put what he wanted to say into words.

"Zill. You know that's not true. The barn roof, the farm – it's all for you. What else d'you think we work for? It's *your* future, girl. We'll hand this farm to you, just like my father handed it to me, just like you'll hand it on to your children. That's what it's all about, isn't it?"

"It's not my future!" yelled Zillah. "I don't want it! You don't understand. No one does except Great-aunt Zillah."

She rushed out, slamming the door. I listened to her feet banging up the stairs, then far away her bedroom door crashed open, then shut. She wasn't going to come down again, I knew it. I was alone with Geoff the Murderer, and Angry Janice.

Chapter Fourteen

Except that Janice wasn't angry, and Geoff didn't look like a murderer.

"Oh dear," said Janice. "What an upset," and she smiled pleadingly at me, as if she was begging me not to have noticed how angry Zillah was.

"She's still not got over it," said her dad. The words startled me, like an echo. For a moment I couldn't think where I'd heard them before, and then I remembered Mrs T saying *Poor little Zillah, she never got over it.*

"Her great-aunt died, you see," Janice explained to me. "Zillah was very fond of her."

"I know," I said, then wished I hadn't when Janice pounced on it.

"Do you? How? Did Zillah tell you about it? She won't ever talk about her great-aunt to us."

"I only wish she would," said Geoff. It was *so convincing.* I nearly opened my mouth and blabbed out everything. The diamond ring, the crushed-up pills, what Mrs T had said: everything. But luckily I stopped myself. Zillah would never trust me again, I knew. And although Janice and Geoff sounded just like any worried mum and dad, I wasn't sure if I could believe them or not. Maybe murderers *are* convincing...

"She *has* talked to you," said Janice. "I know she has. I wish you'd tell us, Katie. All we want to do is to help her."

"Umm, sorry, she hasn't really told me anything," I mumbled guiltily. But whatever I did I was going to feel guilty. Guilty if I didn't keep Zillah's secret, guilty if I did. "I'd better go home. Mum will be expecting me. Thank you for the tea – the cake was great."

"Take a piece home," said Janice eagerly. "Go on, Zillah never eats cake."

Quickly, she wrapped a piece in foil for me. I felt even more guilty when I put it into my backpack. She was being so nice, but all the time I knew...

What did I know?

"Geoff'll walk you down to the cottage. It's a bit late for you to be out on your own."

"Oh no, please don't bother, I'm fine, I always walk home on my own –"

"No," said Janice firmly. "Geoff will take you."

We stepped out into the blustery darkness. Now I was glad the wind was so loud, because I wouldn't have to talk to Geoff. All I had to do was follow the light of his torch, as it bounced up and down on the puddles. But when we got to the cottage, and I was stamping the mud off my feet in the doorway before knocking, he said, "You mustn't mind Zill. She doesn't mean half what she says. She's got things all muddled up inside her, since her great-aunt died. It's good she's got you for a friend."

Suddenly I realized two things:

1) I still didn't know what had really happened to Zillah's great-aunt, but Zillah's dad *does* love her, whatever she thinks.

2) He loves her the same way my dad loved me, in a proper dad way.

I scraped my boots very slowly on the ancient metal door-scraper that must have been there long before Great-aunt Zillah was born. I didn't want Zillah's dad to see my face, because I was afraid I was going to cry.

"S'OK. Thanks for tea," I mumbled, and I bashed on the knocker and hoped Mum would come quickly. All I wanted was to put my arms round Mum and hug her as tight as I could, so I would be sure that she was still there and nothing was ever, ever going to happen to her.

Chapter Fifteen

Wednesday, November 6th

Dear Jessie,

Thank you for telling me who's got my bedroom. I'm glad it's a girl, not a boy. It's funny that she goes to our school. Do you walk to school with her? Don't tell her about the secret hiding-place under the floor-boards, because I left my coin collection in there.

I've got so much to tell you, but I'm going to wait till you come at Christmas. It's much too complicated to put in a letter. You'd think I'm living in a crazy place surrounded by crazy people. (Perhaps that's true...)

I wonder if you'd like Zillah. I'm pretty sure you wouldn't like Susie. I can just see you rolling your eyes when Susie flicks her curls back for the millionth time. You can tell, with Susie, that all the time when she was little a whole crowd of grannies and aunties were standing round her saying, "Ooh, what lovely curls she's got!" And poor old Susie's got stuck like that.

She wants me to go to Guides' pot-luck supper with

her on Saturday, and stay over. Everybody has to bring something to eat, then we all share it and sing songs and tell ghost stories.

Mum says, "That'll be nice, Katie. You'll meet lots of people there. It'll be good for you to make some other friends."

Things you can't do in Cornwall in November:
Go ice-skating (unless you want to go to Truro or somewhere, which takes about two hours).
Go into town with your friends, call in on your friends, phone your friends (unless you have a car which works, and a mum who will drive you everywhere, and a tele-phone).
Go to the cinema   (nearest cinema is 6 miles away).
Go out for a pizza ("   pizza place " " " ").
Go to drama club ("   drama club " " " ").
Go to a pool   ("   swimming pool is I don't know how many miles away).

It's too depressing. Time to make another list. . .

Things you can _do in Cornwall in November:_
Go to Guides' pot-luck supper with Susie, sleep over with Susie and hear lots more about how the Buryans hate the Treliskes.
Maybe walk to the other side of Nancledra to Mark and Bryony's, and see their pony? Mark said even if I'd never ridden a horse before, I'd be fine on Bouncer,

who is old and fat and really friendly. I had a look on the map, and it looks as if I could walk it, if I go straight across the fields without bothering about roads.
See Zillah (who didn't come into school today, so I still don't know if she wants to paint her room or not).
Go on an expedition with Mum. She wants us to walk to somewhere called Botallack where there are ruined tin mines she's desperate to draw.

Jessie, do you remember when we thought Mrs Barnett was really going to call the police, after we picked those flowers of hers that were hanging over the pavement? What do you think it would be like if you really had committed a crime – a serious one – and you were waiting and waiting for someone to find out? Wouldn't it be awful?

How long do you think people go to prison for, if they accidentally do something that hurts another person – maybe even kills them – but they didn't mean to?

I've got to go, Mum's calling.

I'll write again really soon.

Lots of love,

Katie

PS Mum went into St Ives on the bus today and bought me a green waterproof jacket with a hood, a pair of green waterproof trousers, and a huge pair of green wellingtons which come up to my knees. She said there wasn't much choice. It all cost loads of money so I didn't say anything.

Chapter Sixteen

Zillah came back to school today, after two days. I didn't think she was coming, because she wasn't on the school bus, but Janice brought her in the car. I think Janice must have talked to Mr Trevelyan, because he was late coming into our class, and then I saw Janice through the window, hurrying across the playground to her car.

Zillah didn't look good, even though she was supposed to be better. But she smiled as if she was glad to see me, and whispered, "See you in the playground later."

When we went out for break, Zillah didn't bring her book as usual. Instead, she kept close to me, and we went over and sat on the chestnut-tree stump, away from the others. Out in the sunshine, she looked pale.

"I'm glad you're back," I said. "I've missed you."

"Have you?" Zillah looked surprised, then pleased. "I had a horrible headache. Mum made me see the doctor."

"But you're OK now?"

"Yeah. Just tired."

It was nice sitting on the stump in the sun. For the first time, I was glad I wasn't in my old playground, with hundreds of kids rushing round and a noise you can hear three streets away.

Mrs T was in her garden, putting the baby out to sleep in his pram. I didn't call, in case it woke him up, but I waved when she looked up, and she waved back. Then she came over to the playground wall, and beckoned to us. Zillah got up reluctantly, but she got up.

"Hello, you two," said Mrs T. "Isn't it a blissful day? If the weather was always like this I'd be a perfect mother. The kids have been playing out in the garden since seven o'clock and now they're too tired even to squeak. Luckily, I recorded *Playdays*. Are you feeling better, Zillah?"

She said it very kindly. I thought of what Mrs T had said about being down at the cottage with Zillah and her great-aunt. She must have known Zillah well.

Zillah didn't scowl, or duck her head down, the way she often did when Mr Trevelyan spoke to her. She smiled a little pale smile, and said, "How's baby Josh?"

"Not such a baby now. It's absolute ages since I've talked to you, Zillah. You must come and see the kids. Do you remember how you used to cuddle Josh?"

"Yes," said Zillah.

"You were marvellous with him. What was that song you used to sing to him?"

"It was silly," said Zillah. "It was a song for a girl, really, not for a boy. Great-aunt Zillah – Great-aunt Zillah used to sing it to me when I was little."

"I think I can remember it," said Mrs T, and she began to sing in a light, clear voice:

"*She was as beautiful as a butterfly*
And proud as a Queen
Was pretty little Polly Perkins
Of Paddington Green..."

"Paddington Green!" I said. "That's in London."

"Yes," said Mrs T thoughtfully. "It doesn't sound like a Cornish song."

"My great-aunt Zillah went to London," said Zillah. "She went there in the war. She worked for a year in an aircraft factory."

"Did she!" said Mrs T. "I never knew that."

They were silent, both of them, remembering. After a while Mrs T said, "I must get the washing on. Remember, Zillah, come and see me soon. And you too, Katie." And she hurried back into the house.

"She's nice," I said.

Zillah nodded.

"She really liked your great-aunt Zillah."

"They used to play chess together," said Zillah. "Mrs T was always coming down to our place."

Our place? I was pretty sure she didn't mean the farm.

"You mean the cottage?"

"Of course," said Zillah, surprised that I could have thought she meant anywhere else. "I was down the cottage most of the time when I was little. My mum and dad had to work."

"On the farm?"

"That's right. You should have seen the state it was in when my dad inherited it. He did everything, built up the herd. The old farm was all he thought about. But then there was the trouble with BSE and everything got knocked down again."

"And your mum helped."

"She worked full-time. That's why she sent me down to Great-aunt Zillah's. I told you before, all they really care about is the farm."

She was looking miserable again. I wished I hadn't started asking questions.

"I wish I'd met your great-aunt Zillah," I said.

"I put flowers on her grave," said Zillah. "I make sure she's always got fresh flowers."

"That's nice."

"Yeah. She loved flowers."

Then the bell rang, and we all went in.

* * *

The school bus was late back. It was quite exciting, because there'd been a mud-slide and a whole load of stones and mud had fallen over the road. A tractor was trying to move it. We all said we'd go and help, but they wouldn't let us. Someone said a digger had been sent for from Penzance. Our driver didn't know whether to go back, and try another route round, which would have taken about half-an-hour longer, or wait. We all wanted him to wait, because it was quite exciting once the digger came, with all the flashing lights and great loads of mud and rock being lifted and dumped. Everyone started sharing out sweets and stuff, and talking about times when there'd been floods or snowstorms before. It sounded great, and I began to look forward to the winter. Some days, Mark told me, the school bus can't get through at all. He told me about the time when he and Bryony went to school on Bouncer, taking turns to ride. When they got there, they put him in the paddock next to Mr Trevelyan's garden.

"I wish I could ride to school one day," I said longingly. Mark said he and Bryony would come over on Bouncer at the weekend, so I could have a go. "Bouncer's so soft, one of Mr Trevelyan's kids could ride him." Mark knows now that our van doesn't work. Mum reckons she'll be able to afford the new carburettor in about two weeks' time, when she gets the next lot of rent from our London house. And then we'll be able to go anywhere we like. . .

The bus lurched, and we were off again. After I'd said goodbye to Zillah at the farm I raced down the lane, in case Mum was worried. But she wasn't, because she had no idea what time it was. She was playing the radio loudly, and the studio floor was covered with used coffee cups. She had taped her sketches on to the floor and she was walking round and round them, planning her painting. Her hair was pinned up on top of her head and she looked –

Happy.

"Had a good day?" I asked.

"Unbelievable!" Mum said. "I think I've worked it out – I think I know what I'm doing. Katie, Janice said the fish-and-chip van stops outside the pub at seven o'clock tonight. I'll go up and get some."

"Great. Mum, you know Susie asked me to that Guides thing tomorrow night?"

"Oh yes, lovely, now how are we going to get you over there?"

"I don't really want to go, Mum. I told Susie we were going out already."

"Katie, you really shouldn't lie to people."

"All right, Mum. Next time I'll say, *I could come, because I'm not doing anything else, but your Guides' supper sounds unbelievably boring.* Would that be better?"

"Hmm, I suppose not... Mind your feet, Katie, let me move this sketch –"

I left her in peace. Fish-and-chips, Mark and Bryony coming over on Bouncer, maybe getting the paint for Zillah's room –

The weekend was shaping up well.

I thought it was Mum, with her arms full of fish-and-chips, when I heard the banging on the door. I'd put the bolt across, because Mum told me to.

"Coming, Mum!"

But it was Janice who burst into the room and stared round wildly.

"Where is she?"

"Who?"

"Zillah, of course!"

"But Zillah's not here."

Janice looked round again, as if Zillah might be hiding somewhere.

"She must be here. She came to tea with you, didn't she?"

"No, I'm sorry, I haven't seen her since we got off the school bus."

"Off the school bus! But she told me she was coming to tea with you. She said your mother was going to walk her back up the lane at six o'clock."

"Zillah hasn't been here. Really, she hasn't. You can ask Mum."

"Where's Maggie? Is she in the studio?"

"No, she's gone up to the fish-and-chip van."

"I must have just missed her. Listen, Katie. This is serious. Tell me the truth and I won't be cross with you. *Where is Zillah?*"

"I don't know, I really don't know. I'm not lying!"

It was a bit frightening. Janice looked as if she'd like to shake me like a money-box, until the coins flew out. Then suddenly the anger went out of her and she flopped down in one of our kitchen chairs.

"Where can she be? She hasn't been well, she's been upset. I've got to find her."

I tried to think. The boathouse? But why would Zillah go there in the dark? And the path was dangerous at night. Could she have got a bus into St Ives, or Penzance, or St Just?

"Tell me exactly where you last saw her," Janice said.

I thought back. Zillah and I had got off the school bus, and come down the lane as far as the farm. But had she turned in at the farm gate? We'd said goodbye, I remembered that. But I'd been in a hurry, because of Mum, and the bus being late. Maybe Zillah *hadn't* turned in at the gate...

"I'm not sure," I said at last. "We were in the lane, by the farm, but I can't remember if Zillah went in or not. I was in a hurry, because the bus was late."

"How late?"

"It was quarter to five when we got off. I looked at my watch, because of Mum."

"Not quite dark, then," said Janice.

"No, it wasn't dark."

Janice jumped up and began to pace around the table. "I must get Geoff. He'll have to go out looking for her –"

And then to my huge relief, the door opened and in came Mum, with a carrier-bag of fish-and-chips. She took one look at Janice and knew something was seriously wrong.

"It's Zillah!" I said. "She's run away."

"Run away? Janice, what's happened?"

Janice explained, her words stumbling over each other. Mum was suddenly quick and decisive. She put the bag down on the table, and said to Janice, "Come on, we need a telephone. Let's all get up to the farm. Katie, get your coat and boots and bring the fish-and-chips. You'll want something to eat."

Then Mum put her arm round Janice and hugged her.

"It's OK," she said. "Zillah's going to be fine, I know it. First thing is to tell Geoff, then we'll search around the farm and the lane in case she's fallen somewhere and hurt herself. Let me see, it's – what? – nearly half-past seven. So she's been gone for a couple of hours."

"*Nearly three hours*," said Janice.

"All right. Once we're at your place we can work out what to do. Geoff may have had a message by now, to say she's at a friend's house. You need to ring round the village first, in case she's safe somewhere, watching TV."

"But she won't be. Zillah never goes to anyone's house."

"There's always a first time," said Mum. "Right, Katie, we need the big torch and then we're off." She was so calm. I felt really proud of her, and somehow sure that, as she said, we would find Zillah soon.

Chapter Seventeen

Two hours later, I wasn't so sure. I was beginning to get frightened, even though I tried to shut my mind to the things which might have happened to Zillah. She'd be back in the morning, reading her book in the playground. But she was out there now, somewhere, in the dark night...

Everybody in the village was out looking for her. They wouldn't let me help. Children had to stay indoors.

"It's better if you stay here," Mum said. Her face was creased with worry as she flipped through Janice's address book and rang more and more numbers. "Katie, I mean it! Don't go out."

It was horrible, waiting, doing nothing, jumping every time the phone rang. It was horrible being in Zillah's house, without Zillah. I went upstairs, on to the landing, and looked out of the window that faced south, towards the sea. Down in the lanes, I could see lights moving. People were shining torches into ditches and hedges, in case Zillah might have fallen there. Jeeps and tractors criss-crossed the fields slowly, their headlights blazing. You wouldn't believe so many people could get together so quickly. It was like something on TV. Far away, down on the cliff path, more lights flickered. They were going down to the boathouse, to see if Zillah was there, with *Wayfarer*. But I felt sure she wouldn't be. I had the strangest feeling deep inside, almost as if someone was trying to tell me something, but I couldn't quite hear it.

I came slowly downstairs, and sat in Janice's big kitchen. The door banged open and shut and people hurried in and out, with torches and blankets and mobile phones and big, muddy boots. Janice sat at the table with Mum, by the phone, and now there was a policewoman sitting with them, talking and writing things down. Geoff had called the police an hour ago, once we knew that Zillah wasn't in anybody's house, safely watching TV. Now he was out with one of the search parties.

"Wait for the police, Geoff," Janice had said. "They'll want to talk to us."

"I can't sit here. Not while our Zill's out there."

The policewoman was telling Mum and Janice not to worry, lots of kids go missing. "They frighten everybody to death and then they turn up and ask for their tea." Then she started asking hundreds of questions. What was Zillah wearing? Who were her friends? Could Janice remember what Zillah had said in the morning, before she went to school?

It went on and on. It made Zillah sound not like Zillah at all, but like someone you hear about on TV. Janice couldn't remember what colour skirt Zillah was wearing.

"It was her blue denim skirt. No, it can't have been. Her denim skirt was in the wash, I took it out in case the colour ran into the sheets. Oh God, I can't remember."

I didn't really want to interrupt. I didn't want the policewoman to notice me too much. But − they had to know what Zillah was wearing −

"She was wearing her tracksuit," I said. "The dark-blue one."

"Are you sure?" asked the policewoman sharply.

"Yes. Her dark-blue tracksuit, and she had a white T-shirt on underneath. She took her tracksuit top off in the classroom, because it was hot."

"Can you remember her shoes?" the police-woman asked me.

"She'd have been wearing her trainers," Janice cut in. "With that tracksuit, she always wore her trainers."

I frowned, trying to remember. There was something wrong...

"No," I said slowly. "She wasn't... I'm sure she wasn't." Then I saw it in my mind. Zillah, sitting by me in the playground, on the tree stump. I could see her legs in the navy-blue tracksuit trousers, and her heavy dark-brown boots.

"She was wearing her boots," I said. "The brown ones."

"She wouldn't have worn them. They're for walking, not for school," said Janice.

"But she was. I'm sure she was."

The policewoman had turned right round now, facing me.

"You're sure about all this, Katie?"

"Yes."

"She'd have had her trainers on," Janice repeated.

"If Katie says she's sure, then she is," Mum broke in. "She's got an excellent visual memory." I wasn't too sure what this meant, but it sounded all right. At least, it sounded as if I wasn't trying to lie. At least Mum believed me. Janice was looking angry, and the way the policewoman stared and wrote everything down made me feel like a criminal. But I hadn't done anything wrong. I was telling the truth.

"It's all right, Katie," said Mum. She stood up and put her arm round me. "She's a bit upset," she said to the policewoman.

"Katie, you're a friend of Zillah's, aren't you?" said the policewoman. "I know you want to help us to find out where she is, as soon as we can. And it looks as if you were the last person who saw her this afternoon. It's very important that you tell me everything you remember. Everything. Even if it seems silly, or not very important."

She took me through every detail of the bus journey home from school. Where we'd sat, what we'd talked about. But we hadn't really talked at all, even though I'd sat next to Zillah. I told the policewoman about the mud-slide and us being late, and everything.

Then the policewoman asked me about getting off the bus. Who were we with, did we speak to anyone else, did I notice anyone I didn't know, were there any cars in the lane? Anything unfamiliar at all?

My heart was thumping. The more questions she asked, the more it sounded as if something bad had happened to Zillah. *Anything unfamiliar at all.* Someone we didn't know, waiting in the lane. Someone watching. And it was my fault. I hadn't stayed with Zillah. I'd shouted, "Bye! See you tomorrow," or something like that. I couldn't even remember. And then I'd run off down the lane, without looking back.

"I don't know," I kept saying.

That was when the back door opened and Mrs T came in. She was on her own. No babies, no Mr Trevelyan. She saw the policewoman talking to me and stayed over by the door, waiting.

"Tell me, Katie," said the policewoman. She had a

round, smiley face, but it wasn't smiling now. It was heavy and serious. "You haven't known Zillah very long, but her mum says you're her only real friend. She says Zillah talks to you."

I didn't know what to say.

"If Zillah *did* talk to you, it's very important that you don't try to keep her secrets. We need to find her quickly. I think Zillah may have been upset about something. Am I right?"

I stared at the policewoman. Upset about something...! But how could I begin? How could I tell the policewoman about Geoff the Murderer and Angry Janice, and the dirty diamonds, and the way Great-aunt Zillah died? She would think I was mad. Or even worse, she would think I was telling the truth, and that would be the end of Zillah's family. They might even send Geoff to prison. And there was Janice sitting at the kitchen table, looking desperate as well as angry, hanging on to every word I said.

Red was flooding up my cheeks. The policewoman stared hard into my eyes, as if she could see through them, into the frightened noise inside my head.

"It's important, Katie. It's important for Zillah. You want to help us to find her, don't you?"

"Of course I do!" I said, louder than I meant. "I don't know where she is, I've told you millions of times that I don't know and Zillah didn't tell me anything."

But the policewoman wasn't leaving it there. "Katie," she said, "I think you know something that you're not telling me. Perhaps you'd like to go somewhere more private." And she glanced round at Janice.

"No," I said. "I don't want to go anywhere. I don't know anything. Zillah never said anything to me about running away."

"Running away?" said the policewoman. "What makes you think she's run away?"

"Because she's not here, is she!" I shouted. I saw her face go still, not angry, but satisfied somehow, as if she *wanted* me to shout at her, as if she *wanted* me to lose control. And now I'd done it. Mum reached out her hand, but I knew if I took it I would start to cry and I wouldn't be able to stop. I got up and shoved my chair back. I had to get away. The questions were tangling in my head, round and round. Zillah was out there, and that was what mattered. I had to find Zillah. But when I got to the back door, Mrs T was standing in front of it.

I didn't try to push past her. I found myself clinging on to her, as if she was the only person who might be able to help. She knew Zillah. She knew Great-aunt Zillah. She knew how all this had started.

"It's OK, Katie," said Mrs T. "Come with me. We'll go for a walk, just you and me."

Somehow I had my coat on. I didn't dare look at Mum, or the policewoman, or Janice. Mrs T helped me find my boots. I couldn't see properly, even though I'd stopped myself from crying.

"We'll be back in a mo," she called back, and the door was shut, and we were out in the cool dark.

"Let's go this way," she said, "down to the cottage. I could walk this lane blindfold."

I could hear distant shouts, and the churning of car engines and tyres. But Mrs T didn't seem to notice any of it.

"So peaceful," she said. "No wonder Zillah loved it."

I didn't ask her which Zillah she meant.

Her voice went on quietly in the darkness, remembering. "She used to collect little Zillah from the farm at six o'clock in the morning, so Janice and Geoff could get on with the milking. Little Zillah was down there all day long, then if it was getting late she'd stay the night. Janice absolutely hated it when little Zillah started calling the cottage 'home'. She'd say, 'I want to go home,' when Geoff brought her back to the farm."

"So ... really ... Great-aunt Zillah was a bit like Zillah's mum?"

"Yes," said Mrs T, "I think she was. You have to

remember that, Katie. Losing a great-aunt doesn't sound too awful, does it? But when that person has practically been your mother, really ... poor Zillah."

We were nearly at the cottage. I could hear the wind and the sea, and I thought of Zillah out in it somewhere, in the dark, with only her jacket and her school backpack, alone. If Mrs T was right, then Zillah was like me. Losing Great-aunt Zillah was like me losing Dad. Only it was worse for Zillah, because no one had understood how she felt. I thought of all the flowers and cards people had sent to me and Mum when Dad died. Even though they didn't really make any difference, I'd kept all the cards. I wondered if anyone had sent cards to Zillah.

Zillah hadn't had anyone to talk to. Only me. Angry Janice, Geoff the Murderer, Scowling Zillah... But it wasn't so funny when you were trapped inside it, like Zillah. Zillah, alone in her horrible bedroom, thinking about the same thing over and over. Her dad, crushing up the pills. And the next day, Great-aunt Zillah was dead, when Zillah believed she was getting better.

"She thought −" I began.

"Mm?" Mrs T sounded interested, but not in the same way as the policewoman. She didn't sound as if she was going to rush off and write down everything I said. And it was dark, so she couldn't see my face. Mrs T had brought her big torch, but she hadn't switched it on.

"She thinks – Zillah thinks that her dad murdered Great-aunt Zillah."

Mrs T was silent for a long time. I couldn't see her face. Then she said, "How?"

"He crushed up some tablets and gave them to her, the night before she died. Zillah saw it. And Zillah said she was getting better before that."

"She wasn't," said Mrs T. "Zillah hoped it was true, but it wasn't. She was getting worse."

"But the tablets..."

"Yes," said Mrs T. "The tablets. I'm sure they were real. I'm sure Zillah saw something. She's not the kind of girl to lie about a thing like that. But –"

"What?"

"Maybe Zillah didn't understand. Maybe Geoff *did* give Great-aunt Zillah some tablets. But he certainly wasn't trying to murder her. He loved her too, you know, even though Zillah doesn't believe it."

"But what was he trying to do?"

"I don't know," said Mrs T slowly. "Only he knows that. She had to take a lot of tablets, you know. But I swear to you, I absolutely swear, that he didn't want to hurt Great-aunt Zillah. If Zillah was here now, I'd tell her exactly the same."

I wouldn't have believed Mrs T if she'd tried to tell me Zillah hadn't seen anything, but I believed her now. Geoff hadn't tried to harm Great-aunt Zillah. He wasn't a murderer. He was just Zillah's dad. It was like a stone rolling off my chest.

"But the question still is, where has she gone?" asked Mrs T.

Suddenly it ran over me, like an electric current. I could hear the words as if Zillah was right next to me, speaking to me. Zillah's voice: "I put flowers on her grave. I make sure she's always got fresh flowers."

"*I think I know where she's gone,*" I said, quietly, as if the wind might hear and carry the words away to Zillah.

"Where?" asked Mrs T, and then we were off, seized by the hope of it, pounding back up the lane.

Chapter Eighteen

But Zillah wasn't there.

Mrs T shone her torch, and I saw the bunch of yellow chrysanthemums in a stone vase, on Great-aunt Zillah's grave.

"She's been here. I'm sure she has."

"Yes."

We both stood staring at the grave. You'd think it might be creepy in a graveyard at night, but it wasn't. The wind had dropped, and it was quiet and calm.

"Dear Zillah," said Mrs T. I knew this time that she was definitely talking about Great-aunt Zillah. She touched the headstone as if she was saying hello to an old friend. "These flowers are fresh, Katie. She must have come here. Look, she's filled the vase with water."

It was so frustrating. Zillah had been there. Maybe if we'd come earlier, we'd have found her.

"Could she be in the church?" I asked.

"It'll be locked at this time. Come on, Katie, let's get you back. I'll get arrested if I keep you out much longer. Oh dear. I felt *so hopeful*. I was sure you were right, and she'd be up here."

I'd felt sure, too. And the strange thing was, that even though there was no Zillah, I still had that feeling of sureness.

"Shine your torch around, *please*."

"Katie, we ought to go –"

"Just once. Please, Mrs T!"

Mrs T lifted her torch and swung it in a slow arc around the walls of the graveyard. It swept from side to side, making shadows, making patterns. All along one wall it went, into the corner, and then along another. Nothing. Mrs T turned.

"I'm terribly sorry, Katie, but I really don't think she's here."

And then, on the third wall, the beam of torchlight hit the side of the hut.

"What's that?"

"Oh, it's just a little hut, where Jos Clodgy keeps the mower – KATIE!"

I was off, stumbling down the path in the dark. She was there, I knew it. And all the old grannies and grandpas and aunties sleeping in the graveyard knew it, too. They wanted me to find her.

I felt for the door of the hut. Mrs T was behind me now, with the torch. A padlock – but it wasn't locked. It hung loose. I slipped off the catch, and the door swung open.

Mrs T shone her torch into the hut. The mower, spades, a clutter of sacks. And in the corner, a dark heap. A curled-up shape. A sleeping-bag.

Zillah.

"Gently," said Mrs T. "We mustn't frighten her."

But the strange thing was that Zillah didn't seem frightened at all. She stirred when the torch shone on her, and then she woke up.

"Zillah, it's me, Katie!" I whispered. I don't know why I was whispering.

"I know it's you," she said. "Is that Mrs T with you?"

"Yes."

"Not Mum and Dad?"

"No."

"Good," said Zillah.

Chapter Nineteen

Mum's lit a fire in my room. It's still burning, even though it's late and everyone's gone to sleep except me. Even Mum's gone to sleep, I think. I could hear her talking downstairs for ages, her and Mrs T and Janice. Janice has gone back to the farm. Zillah's on the camp-bed. I think she's asleep. I'll just have a look. Yes, she's asleep.

There's been so much talking. When we got back we walked straight into three policemen. They'd come up to help with the search, in a police Land Rover. They started sending out messages, then people came crowding in. More messages went out on mobiles to say that Zillah was found, and then more searchers came back. Geoff started splashing whiskey into glasses, Mum and Janice were hugging and crying, and suddenly the farm kitchen was full of clumpy boots and big coats and people shouting over one another's heads. And then Zillah said she wanted to come down to the cottage with me and Mum, and Janice nearly started crying again.

Geoff said, "If that's what's best for Zill, that's what we'll do," and he helped her put her stuff in a bag for overnight. "You'll be all right down there with Katie, won't you, girl." Zillah didn't say much, but she didn't scowl, either. It's so nice to be able to like Geoff without having to keep on trying to work out if he's a murderer or not.

The police are coming back in the morning, to talk to Zillah properly. They talked a bit tonight, but Zillah was too tired. They still don't know about any of the Geoff-the-Murderer stuff.

But Janice does, and so does Mum. Mrs T told them. Mrs T asked me about it first. She said that she thought we'd got to tell Zillah's parents, or it would never get straightened out. I wasn't too sure if it was a good idea, but I know Mrs T cares about Zillah, so I agreed. And I didn't want Zillah to run away ever again.

Because Zillah *was* going to run away. She told me. That's why she wore her walking boots. She was planning to walk all the way into Penzance, miles and miles in the dark, and then catch a train. She'd planned it all. She'd taken her stuff up to the hut the day before, her sleeping-bag and her money and everything. She knew Jos Clodgy only uses the hut on Saturdays, when he mows the graveyard.

But she said she couldn't leave without taking flowers to Great-aunt Zillah. It would have been like going without saying goodbye to her. She put the flowers in the vase, and changed the water, and tidied up the grave a bit. Great-aunt Zillah liked things ship-shape. It was getting dark by then, Zillah said. And she kept thinking she'd set off any minute, but she didn't.

"Sounds stupid, doesn't it, Katie," said Zillah, staring at the warm shadows the fire makes on my bedroom walls. "But it was as if Great-aunt Zillah didn't want me to go. I kept thinking, I've *got* to go, but then I'd remember her saying, 'You keep here with me, Zillah. Don't go running off now.' That's what she used to say when I was little, when we went walking along the cliff-top. She used to let me explore, but she always made sure I was safe. And it was getting darker and darker. So I thought I'd have a rest in the hut, then later on when I wasn't so tired, I'd go. But I fell asleep, and then you came."

I think she was glad I came. Otherwise, she'd still be out there, in the dark night, walking her way to Penzance. It would take hours, at night, and going across the fields. It's raining again now. It makes me shiver to think that Zillah might still be out there. I check the camp-bed again. Yes, she's asleep. Safe, the way Great-aunt Zillah wanted.

Mrs T said to Zillah what she'd said to me, about being sure, absolutely sure, that Geoff would never have done anything to hurt Great-

aunt Zillah. Zillah sat on one side of the table, and
Mrs T on the other, both of them leaning forward.
They stared into each other's faces as if there
wasn't anyone else in the room. I didn't move. I
don't think I even breathed.

"I don't doubt what you saw, Zillah," said Mrs T.
"You saw your dad giving Great-aunt Zillah those
tablets. You saw him crushing them up so she could
swallow them."

"Yes," said Zillah. "I know I did."

"But what you saw wasn't the whole story," said
Mrs T. "You saw a little bit, not enough to understand. She needed those tablets. She was in pain and
she couldn't settle. Your dad knew it. He was looking after her, Zillah. He was doing his best for her.
He would never have hurt Great-aunt Zillah. You
know your dad. Family's everything to him."

Zillah stared at Mrs T. I knew she wanted to
believe her.

"Are you sure?" she whispered.

"I'm sure," said Mrs T.

Zillah looked different, after Mrs T said that. Her
face changed, and she yawned and then shivered all
over, as if she was shaking something off. Mrs T
said, "Don't think about it any more tonight, Zillah."
And she dug around in the pocket of her waterproof,
and brought out a packet of the kind of C-H-O-C-O-
L-A-T-E B-I-S-CU-I-T-S that are so expensive they

only sell them in special shops. I know, because Mum buys them on my birthday.

"My secret supply," she said. "I have to keep them locked up." And she gave the packet to Zillah and me.

Chapter Twenty

The fire was white ash when I woke up, and the sun was shining on the opposite wall. The curtains were pulled back, and Zillah's camp-bed was empty. I sat up. Everything that had happened the night before rushed back into my mind. From downstairs, I heard the murmur of voices. Mum's, and Zillah's.

They were in the studio. I didn't want to interrupt, so I crept past and out into the garden. It was very still, and the sun was almost warm. I went down the path through the nettles to the outside toilet. (Already it feels as if we've been living here for years. I can hardly remember what it was like to have a proper bathroom inside the house.)

The biggest spider in the universe was sitting on the closed toilet seat. I jumped backwards, and banged my head on the door-frame. The spider waved a leg at me.

"I suppose you think you're very clever," I said. "I bet you think I won't dare move you off that toilet seat. You think I'm going to go running off to get Mum, don't you?"

The spider waved another leg. Yes, that was definitely what it thought.

"You're wrong," I said. "You're *so* wrong." I looked around to see what I could use. There was nothing inside the toilet. But outside, growing near to the nettles, there were some big, tough dock leaves. One of those would do perfectly. I picked it, and hid it behind my back.

I walked up to the spider very slowly. I was so close I could see the little hairs on its legs. It was the closest I'd ever come to a spider, without running away. But this time I was staying. Very slowly and gently, so as not to let the spider guess what I was planning, I brought the dock leaf out from behind my back. The spider had stopped waving its legs now, and was looking puzzled.

"You thought I was going to run away, didn't you?" I said. Keep talking, I thought. Distract its attention. "Well, you were wrong. Don't worry, I'm not going to hurt you. But I think it's about time you realized who this toilet belongs to..." and I slid the dock leaf under the spider, lifted it, and carried it outside the door. The spider was so surprised it did nothing. It sat tight on its plate of leaf.

"Here you are. This is *your* place, out in the

garden. And don't pick any more fights, because I'm going to win."

I laid the dock leaf down in a dry spot under some ivy leaves. The spider looked at me again, and waved its legs. I knew what it was saying this time: *OK. You win.*

I went back inside the toilet, and shut the door.

Strangely enough, Zillah and Mum weren't very interested when I started telling them about the Great Spider Victory. But then, neither of them is afraid of spiders. Zillah was drawing with Mum's pastels. Mum must have been up early, because there were drawings all over the floor already. Most of them were of the garden, looking like a deep pool of long grass, weeds and sun. She'd drawn loads of sketches of the outside toilet, too. Why, Mum, why? We don't need to advertise it!

"Look at the way the sunlight falls on the whitewash," Mum was saying. "Quite Mediterranean, even with the sun so low in the sky. Look at the tone of those shadows, Zillah."

And Zillah was looking.

"Your hand is too tense," Mum went on. "Loosen up. Sweep that line across. You're drawing, not writing."

Zillah's hand moved across the paper. The marks were getting surer, stronger.

"That's good," said Mum. "You're getting there. Oh, Katie, I forgot all about breakfast."

We ate breakfast in the garden, in our jackets, in the November sun. I scrambled some eggs, and Mum made hot chocolate for us. Zillah didn't say anything at all about running away, or her parents. We sat in the sun and talked about Mum's work, and how maybe Zillah could come down to the studio and have drawing lessons, and whether Bryony and Mark really would come over with Bouncer later on. Then Mum poured her third cup of coffee, and broke the spell.

"Time to go up to your mum and dad's soon, Zillah," she said. "They're waiting for you."

"How do you know?" Zillah asked. It didn't sound rude, it sounded as if she really wasn't sure.

"Your mum was down here before it was light," said Mum, "asking how you'd slept, whether you were all right. She couldn't keep away."

Zillah flushed. "I didn't hear her," she said.

"You were fast asleep. She didn't want to wake you."

"Oh," said Zillah.

"And your dad wants to talk to you. He wants to tell you what really happened."

"He'll be so angry!" said Zillah.

"No," said Mum, "he's not angry. He's just glad you're home safe."

"And the police. Will I have to talk to them?" asked Zillah, looking frightened.

"Just a bit."

It was very quiet. A bee buzzed down to the ivy flowers, and the dogs barked up at the farm.

"I'll go then," said Zillah.

"Do you want me to come with you?" asked Mum.

"No," said Zillah. "I'll go on my own. I'll go on up now."

And she did. I was a bit worried about it, just in case... But Mum seemed quite sure that Zillah would go straight home, and she was right. Zillah told me bits of what happened, not all at once, but when we were busy with other things, like sanding a rough bit on one of *Wayfarer*'s oars, or planting spring bulbs on Great-aunt Zillah's grave, or biking over to visit Mark and Bryony.

Geoff had crushed the tablets up because Great-aunt Zillah had suddenly started to have trouble swallowing. He'd mixed them in a drink to help her. She was in pain, and he knew she needed them straight away. As Mrs T had said, she was on a lot of tablets. And then, in the night, she'd had another stroke. But the stroke didn't happen because of the tablets, Zillah's dad was sure of that. It would have happened anyway.

That was how Great-aunt Zillah had died. They

hadn't explained any of the details to Zillah, because they didn't want to upset her. She'd been so sure her great-aunt was getting better.

"So they just told me Great-aunt Zillah was in heaven, and she was happy," said Zillah. "That's the kind of thing you say to a baby, not to someone who's nearly nine, like I was."

"I know. But people say weird things, when someone dies," I said.

"Weird," Zillah agreed. She sounded so much happier. Now that the weight of believing those terrible things about her dad had lifted, I could see how heavy it had been. Going over and over in her mind what she'd seen. Her dad crushing up the tablets, and feeding them to Great-aunt Zillah. Great-aunt Zillah lying in bed the next morning, still and cold. I knew that Zillah had seen her when she was dead, because she told me. *I had to say goodbye to her, Katie. I wanted to see her.*

I thought about Dad. I wished I'd been able to say goodbye to him properly, not in the rush and panic of the ambulance coming and no one being able to believe what had happened. Not in the hospital either. By that time he didn't really look like Dad any more. He was too far away from us.

"You OK?" Zillah asked.

"Yeah. Just thinking about something. What about your diamond ring, Zill?"

"Dad said he was going to put it in the bank for me, until I was older. Then I could decide if I wanted to sell it to pay for my education, or keep it."

"What did you say?"

"What do you think?"

"Keep it?"

"Yeah, I was going to," said Zillah thoughtfully. "But then I remembered that Great-aunt Zillah always said to me, 'That's for your future, girl.' And I began to wonder if she really meant for me just to wear it – or if it was for something else."

"So what are you going to do?"

"I asked Dad to get it valued. He took it up to Truro. And –" Zillah paused, watching me.

"And?"

"The jewellers he showed it to said it should be sent up to London for valuation."

"Are you going to?"

"We have. Dad got the letter today."

"Zillah! Why don't you just *tell* me?"

"Thirty thousand pounds."

I was silent. Zillah looked at me, and a smile curled round her face.

"I didn't believe it either, till Dad showed me the letter. It's been in the family such a long time we were just used to it. Great-aunt Zillah had it from her mother, and she had it from her granny. We knew it was diamonds, but we never thought of it being worth anything like that much."

"Thirty thousand pounds. Wow."

So it wasn't the engagement ring Susie Buryan had told me about. Susie and her mouth. She always reckons she knows everything about everyone, but *no one* knows everything about everyone. Think of all the secrets there are, just in a normal family. Let alone Zillah's family...

"And you had it on a string round your neck at school. What if it'd fallen off and you'd lost it? *Thirty thousand pounds.*"

"I think Great-aunt Zillah knew all the time. I think that's why she said, 'Keep hold of that ring, Zillah. That's for your future.'"

"So what are you going to do?"

"Sell it," said Zillah slowly. "We need the money. Dad says it's all got to go for my education, and my future, like Great-aunt Zillah wanted. But I think some of it should go for other things. It wouldn't be right, would it, Katie? Me with thirty thousand pounds, and Mum and Dad scratting round to pay the next feed bill. Half the reason Mum shouts all the time is because she's worried. Great-aunt Zillah wouldn't want that. Dad won't hear of using the money except for my education, he says, but I'm going to keep on till he gives in."

She looked as fierce and Zillah-ish as ever. I

really didn't think Geoff had much of a chance against her.

"Dad wants me to go to agricultural college when I'm eighteen," Zillah went on.

"But you don't like farming."

"No," said Zillah. "But it's going to take Mum and Dad a long time to get round to understanding that I really want to be an astrophysicist, isn't it?"

"Astrophysicist! Zillah!"

"You believed me! You believed me!" Zillah screamed with laughter, and I tried to slap her with a roller covered in yellow paint, but she dodged out of my way.

"I'll get you next time," I promised. "Zillah, you'll have to go over that bit again. See those pale patches? You've got to get it even."

We were painting Zillah's room yellow. It had been hard to find just the right yellow, not too harsh and not too dark, but not too pale and girly either. Mum drove us into Penzance (the van's got a new carburettor from a salvage place) and she spent ages trying out little sample paint-pots on pieces of lining paper. But at last we got the right shade. Zillah thought we were crazy.

"You'll see what a difference it makes, when the room's finished," Mum promised. "It doesn't matter how much time it takes, as long as we get the perfect yellow."

Zillah's bedroom is nearly finished. We did the gloss first, and Janice is making a new blind, from a kit. Blinds are better than curtains, for a north-facing room. But you'd hardly know it was north-facing any more. It's so full of light, and colour. The yellow makes it look as if the sun's shining even when it's not.

"I can't wait to see what it looks like when you get your bookcase back in, and that new hanging wardrobe your dad's making." Geoff has got rid of the old black wardrobe. No one wanted it, so he smashed it up with a chopper and we had a bonfire in the yard. I was really glad to see it go. I never told Zillah, but I thought that wardrobe looked exactly like a big black coffin standing upright. Zillah and I danced round the flames.

"Glad to see the back of that old thing," said Geoff. "I never liked it." He's making a hanging wardrobe with a carved rail, and Zillah's chosen the curtains for it. It's going to look fantastic.

"The only problem is that there won't be anywhere for burglars to hide any more," I said.

Zillah's getting a camp-bed so her friends can sleep over. She says she doesn't ever want anyone staying except me, but I don't believe that's going to last. Things are changing. Mark and Bryony came over again last Sunday, and Zillah talked to both of them. Not a lot, but it was definitely conversation. We both had a ride on Bouncer.

"You'll be going to the Guides' pot-luck supper next," I said, but unfortunately I fell off Bouncer at that point, and Zillah showed no sympathy at all.

Nearly finished. Another half-hour and this wall will be done. My arms are aching but I'm not going to stop now, and nor is Zillah. Mum was right. It's the perfect yellow.

Chapter Twenty-One

Only two more days before we break up. Carol-singing tomorrow, and then it's nearly Christmas. I can't wait to go carol-singing. We're all going to carry lanterns, and meet at the church. First we go all around the village, then on to the outlying farms. The last farm we go to is Eglos Farm, and they always give the carol-singers baked potatoes and mulled wine and mince pies. Everybody comes. I wish it would snow, but I don't think it will. Imagine tramping through the snow with lanterns...

It'll be brilliant at New Year, too. We've all been invited to a fancy-dress party in St Ives, at Mum's friend's studio. Jessie will be staying with us then, so she'll be able to come too. I think Jessie is a bit worried about meeting Zillah. After all, she doesn't know Zillah, except from my letters. And then Jessie has always been my best friend, in London... But I'm not going to worry about that now. Mum says it will be fine. And it's already fixed up that I'm going to London next half-term, to stay with Jessie for a week. I think that will be all right, too, as long as I don't walk past our house and look up at my old bedroom window. As long as I don't look at the place where the lilac tree used to be.

The lilac tree's gone. Mum arranged for it to be cut down. I didn't know, until she told me last week. She said she'd thought and thought about it before she decided, because she and Dad used to love the lilac tree so much. They planted it when they moved into our London house, when I was a baby.

Mum said that she'd decided to have it cut down in the end, because one day we'll go back to our London house, and we'll want to start again. It'll be a new London life, not our old London life. Mum said that when we go back we'll plant another tree, a different tree, in memory of Dad. We'll go to the garden centre together, and choose one.

It was strange when she said "in memory of Dad", because I never think of Dad as a memory. Sometimes he's here, so sharply that it hurts. Other times, I can't find him at all. I can't even remember his face. But I think that's how it is when people die, because I asked Zillah, and she said it was just the same for her.

Dad would like a tree.

I haven't told you about what happened to Mum. She took some of her new work to a gallery-owner in St Ives, and she's going to have a show, with three other painters. It's going to be in May. Mum hasn't had a show for nearly three years, and even then it was only a little one in Camden, with ten other people. She drove the van back at about a million miles an hour, leaped out with a huge box of cream-cakes, turned up the music and danced around the kitchen. Later on, she got really worried and started saying, "I'm not ready for this, Katie. That big landscape needs months of work. What am I going to do? I'll have to phone Robert and tell him I can't do it!" (Robert is the gallery-owner.)

For once, it was lucky that we haven't got a phone. I didn't say anything, because I know Mum. I just ate the cream-cakes. By the next day Mum was feeling better again. She stayed in her studio for about sixteen hours, drinking more coffee than ever, and then she came out and said, "I think it's going to be OK, Katie."

I do, too. When Mum makes up her mind to do something, she usually does it.

And now I'm coming to the last thing I want to tell you. At least, for now. I was on my own in the cottage yesterday. It was about three o'clock in the afternoon, very still and quiet. Mum had gone down to the cove to gather driftwood for our fires. It's amazing what you can find after there's been a gale. Usually I go with her, to help drag the sack of driftwood back up the cliff-path, but yesterday I had some homework to finish. Mr Trevelyan had told us to write two pages from the diary of a girl or a boy who'd lived where we live a hundred years ago. (Jenny Pendour immediately stuck her hand up and said she lived in a bungalow which was built in 1967. Mr Trevelyan said that didn't matter. All she had to do was think about who was living in that place, then. "Do the diary of the cow who used to graze where your house was, Jenny," suggested Bryony.)

I thought it would be easy to write the diary, but it wasn't. I kept starting, then crumpling up the paper and throwing it in the stove, and starting again. The girl whose diary I was pretending to write didn't seem real at all. In the end I gave up.

I was just sitting at the table, thinking about nothing. Then I heard a little sound. So tiny I didn't know what it was, at first. Then it came again, louder.

It was someone laughing. And the strange thing was that the laughter was familiar, like the laughter of someone I knew. I tried and tried to think who it was. You probably won't believe this, but I wasn't at all surprised or frightened, even though I was on my own in the cottage, and there shouldn't have been anyone there to laugh except me.

It was a child laughing. Someone very young, I think. She giggled again, then there was silence for a moment. After the silence another voice came in, an old woman's voice, saying something which I couldn't quite hear. But it made the little girl laugh again. I knew by now it was a little girl. And I almost – almost – knew who it was...

It was Zillah. I heard her voice, saying words I couldn't quite catch, and then her laughter, and Great-aunt Zillah laughing, too. You could tell how happy they were. "*Little Zillah used to be down there at the cottage the whole time. She adored her great-aunt.*" I listened to the two voices. Maybe they were baking a cake together, and Zillah was helping. You could tell they had a lot of jokes together, that no one else knew.

I sat and listened, and little by little the voices and laughter grew quieter and quieter, dying away until there was nothing left but the sound of the stove.

I didn't write about it in the diary for Mr Trevelyan. It would have been like giving away a secret. But I think, one day, I could tell Zillah. I think she'd believe me.